PLEASE HOLD

BY

TRICIA STEWART SHIU

Licensing Notes

TABLE OF CONTENTS

AUTHOR'S NOTE

Dear Readers,

I would like to provide an update regarding the foreword of my novel, PLEASE HOLD. Seven years ago, Mike Hopkins, graciously wrote the foreword for this book. Since then, there have been significant changes in my personal and professional life.

Firstly, I would like to clarify that the mention of my husband in the foreword refers to my ex-husband. Our relationship has since ended, and I wanted to ensure that this information is accurately reflected in the context of the foreword.

Additionally, I want to acknowledge that Mike Hopkins has transitioned from his previous role as CEO of Hulu to his current position as Senior Vice President, Prime Video and Amazon Studios. I congratulate him on this achievement and appreciate his ongoing support for my work.

I believe it is important to provide these updates to maintain accuracy and clarity for readers. Thank you for your understanding, and I hope you enjoy reading PLEASE HOLD.

Warm regards,

Tricia Stewart Shiu

FOREWORD BY MIKE HOPKINS, SENIOR VICE PRESIDENT, PRIME VIDEO AND AMAZON STUDIOS

I've known Tricia and her husband Eric for more than twenty years. And while I knew she was very creative and engaged in many pursuits outside of her work and family life, I had no idea she was such a creative, witty writer. Until my wife, Sheri and I ran into Tricia and her family at the Southeast Book Festival in Los Angeles. My sister, Lisa Doherty, was receiving an award for her book MOTLEY-SEEING STRIPES as were Tricia and her daughter Sydney for IRON SHINTO, the third book in her YA, SciFi, Mystical Adventure Series.

So, when Tricia told me she was writing a novel about the inner workings of the high-level executive assistant world, I was intrigued and had to read it. I wondered how she could possibly write something that would be translatable to anyone other than entertainment industry insiders. After all, she's worked as an executive assistant for some of the most powerful people in the business world—Rupert Murdoch and Chase Carey, to name two — and experienced an environment most people never get to see.

I'm quite familiar with the world of which Tricia writes. Before becoming CEO at Hulu in 2013, I served in various senior roles at Fox. I've been in the entertainment industry for over twenty years and have been watching and working with executive assistants most of my professional life, but I never quite understood the undercurrent and inner workings of the world of high-level gatekeepers. Meetings, calendars and travel all seemed to fall into place and if there was a problem, I rarely saw it.

When I read PLEASE HOLD, it became clear—there was way more going on than I could ever have imaged. I loved PLEASE HOLD and can only hope that Tricia took a lot of creative license, but somehow I am sure that she's captured the real world pressures and reactions of people caught in tough and tricky situations. PLEASE HOLD offers an interesting take on a world most people only view from the outside and it's quite funny, too. Tricia builds the world and then through immersive details and thematic imagery, draws the reader into the dynamic environment, opening the flood gates for maximum experiential effect.

Tricia's novel, PLEASE HOLD, is a refreshing, unique look at how one woman sees the world, how she rises to meet her challenges, fails miserably at times and how she finds guidance within an emotionally turbulent environment.

I was happy to write this foreword because, in a world where people often equate power and success with greed and negativity, Tricia and her writing shine through. PLEASE HOLD is fresh, original and funny and a testament to Tricia's many years of work and her commitment to truth seeking through objectivity. Nothing could be more entertaining than that.

ACKNOWLEDGMENTS

For Wild Patty.

"You can't be brave if you've only had wonderful things happen to you."

- Mary Tyler Moore

CHAPTER ONE –
CLEAR A PATH

"Did you hear about Sarah?"

"No."

The women's voices waft out of the open office directly into my path. I freeze, clutching a ream of paper to my breasts and sidestep toward the linen covered wall.

"She's being downgraded," one of them says, lowering her voice.

"You're kidding," says the other.

"To Building 99!"

They both laugh gleefully, for several seconds, and it sounds like they high five.

I imagine myself sticking my head around the doorway.
"Sarah who?" I would ask, smiling way too broadly, enjoying how they would jump, how they would fumble, how they would be caught in the middle of their nastiness.
I imagine myself sticking a fork in one of Karsen's hazel eyes.

The women speaking are Grace Maletor and Karsen Baker. Two people who, up to this point, I thought were my friends. We'd have lunch together, and occasionally would sit in each other's offices and gossip when the boss was away. It never occurred to me that I would be one of the topics up for discussion.

I hear the squeak of a chair sliding back and footsteps. My breath seems stopped between my gut and my pancreas and I try to pretend I'm small, smaller than my 5'8" height, and that I possess a magical ability to blend in with the linen wall covering. I close my eyes and wait for an accusing voice, but after a moment the chair slides again, and I hear a creak as someone's backside meets the seat.

Building 99 is so far away executives are issued golf carts. Assistants get to walk. Being sent to Building 99 is like being exiled. What the hell!

I open my eyes again. Checking behind me to make sure no one else is in the hallway, I take a step closer to the doorway. I've learned to glean my information wherever and whenever I can.

"Sarah and Lance have to leave by Friday. I heard that from Marsha," says Karsen, and I can almost see the satisfied smirk on her face.

My boss, Lance Cheroux, is Executive Vice President (EVP) of Worldwide Feature Production, KRG Studio. KRG, is one of the top five studios in Los Angeles, which produces billion dollar grossing feature films, Emmy-winning television shows and multiplatform digital content. Mr. Cheroux is one of five, top tier EVPs, who is being groomed to become President of his division. Because of this, Mr. Cheroux has been reporting directly to the CEO. Marsha Keener's boss is President of Domestic Feature Production, which makes her one level above me.

Levels determine everything about my job, including my inclusion in the company directory. People read that directory like some people read the obituaries but, instead of noticing who is older or younger, it is who is higher or lower on the company totem pole. The only difference is, executives in the Entertainment industry can be resurrected. I remember when any title above a vice president was considered important. But, president titles are a dime a dozen in our business.

And *Friday*! Today is Wednesday, for crying out loud.

Karsen gives one last comment. "Serves her right, Sarah Marks could do with being taken down a few notches. You know she's crazy."

Even though I can't see them, I can feel Grace lean in, both women's heads almost touching. Karsen's hisses, "—sent to a loony farm."

"Why?"

"Almost killed a man. She got so angry she couldn't control herself."

My face grows hot, and for a moment I think I am already in motion, moving toward a confrontation that's been coming a long time, but in reality I have slipped off my heels and am moving back down the hallway as quietly as I can, running toward the Ladies' Room where I can repeatedly flush the toilet while I cry.

Relieved that the restroom is empty, I rush into a stall and sit down on the toilet.

This is the only place I am ensured privacy.

Staring into the bowl through my legs, I imagine my career, my reputation and my sanity pouring out of me into the shimmering water below. Even though I'm alone, I can feel my parents screaming voices—one on either side. I'm five years old. In the background, the TV blares with the "Mary Tyler Moore Show" and I am in the middle, unable to move or speak.

"I can't take this anymore..." My mother holds me tightly in front of her and screams at him, although her words go directly into my right ear.

"You've already ruined Sarah for life." My drunken father slurs, "She'll end up just as crazy as you."

My father grabs my mother and shoves her into a glass plant stand sending it crashing down—narrowly missing me. Frightened for my life, I grab the closest heavy object—an iron trivet—and heave it up. The metal disk clips my father's left temple and sends him hurling toward us face first. Terrified, my mother and I scramble out of the room.

The sound of the outside restroom door opening brings me back to the real world/toilet stall. I'm safely locked in.

The footsteps stop at the sink and I hear someone brushing her teeth. I envision my world as one big bathroom stall, with a shiny sliding lock and six-inch gap at the floor and the ceiling— a veiled illusion of safety and privacy. Shaking off the madness, I straighten my skirt, flush the toilet—and watch my insanity swirl toward the sewer. Then I push the stall door open hard.

As I trudge down the hall toward my office, I focus on the only thing I can at this point—my trivet in the glass-filled plant stand that is my life—the Truth. Sometimes people need a whack upside the head to wake them up. I call this a "Trivet of Truth." Although, I'm not sure it did any good with my father, I still have to wonder, with so many versions of the "truth," which one is real?

Here is the truth about being an executive assistant at a studio. 1) The Entertainment Business is a small world: People move from studio to studio and rank and reputation mean everything. 2) Be nice to everyone: The assistant you snub today could be the executive that fires you tomorrow. 3) There are three types of assisting jobs: First Class, Business Class and Stowaway.

First Class is cushy and includes perks (your own office, kitchen and bathroom, free DVD's and movie premiere passes), one boss (you'd think that would be a given), a parking spot close to the building and—this is key—your own mobile phone. The phone allows a certain amount of, well, mobility.

The Stow Away is a tortuous job which includes no perks, shared offices, community kitchens, community printers, three or more bosses, and worst of all parking in the Green lot.

I'm Business Class. This position is sandwiched between Stowaway and First Class, top tier assistants with VPs, Senior VPs (SVP) and Executive VPs (EVPs) scrambling to get ahead or just digging in to stay where they are in the thickly layered executive totem pole hierarchy.

Stay in the Entertainment industry long enough and you will see a beautiful tapestry of firings and hirings woven into the days, months and years. One moment, an executive rises to the top, revered as the next Leonardo Da Vinci of the modern world, in the blink of an eye, he is a velvet Elvis painting. The word "he" is used because I can count the number of female executives at the studio on one hand that have made it past the EVP level to the "holy grail" title of President. But, fret not, those who rise, can rise again. An executive can be ousted from one studio, and reemerge from the ashes several years later at that same studio or they could dissolve into production deal obscurity.

Understanding that "Today's garage sale art could be tomorrow's Sotheby's masterpiece" has had a profound effect on my work and has given me a depth of understanding about my place in this eternal cesspool dubbed "Entertainment."

This time, I don't hear a soul as I pass by the fateful spot on which I'd stood frozen just fifteen minutes earlier. Karsen has gone back to her desk and Grace yells a quick "hello" as I pass. I say nothing and quicken my pace.

An invisible magnetic force pulls me toward my desk chair.

If I had a mobile phone, I am sure I would no longer feel quite the same attachment to my desk but, it looks like I'm moving further and further in the away from the coveted Presidential Executive Assistant post.

Mr. Cheroux is agitated as he talks to an unidentifiable person, "... How should I know? Six months? I held up my end and there has been no return. None!" His voice drops to a murmur and all I can hear is, "Trebacken."
Six months for what? Is that how much longer he'll be at the company? Souring my
emails and then Mr. Cheroux's, I find absolutely no evidence of what might warrant such a severe location change or why he would be given six months. Then I search Treabacken/Trebachen/Trubachen and Trubacken. Nada. At least, I think he was referring to his job. That's the trouble with overhearing, you're never quite sure of what anything means.
I don't dare ask anyone, for fear of feeding the rumor mill. Digging around for tiny pieces of data is not my favorite thing to do, but it is the only way I am able to gather any concrete information. Before I do any more detective work, Helen from office planning raps tentatively on my door.
"Hi." I say flatly.

"So you've heard." Helen says softly looking down at her nude pumps.

Suddenly, Lance Cheroux calls loudly from his desk, "Hi Helen. You here about the move?"
He knew? I cannot believe this, was I the only person who had no idea I was moving?

"Yes," Helen answers him as she walks into his lush office. There is a bank of windows, which offers a spectacular view of the Pacific Ocean, his leather-topped desk with a handpainted credenza, which holds 2 Oscars, an Emmy and a 3 Tony's behind him.

"Sarah, would you please bring us some coffee?" He places his hand at the small of Helen's back and escorts her to an extra long black leather couch.

As I prepare Mr. Cheroux's coffee—two sugars and a splash of non-fat milk and Helen's—full pour of half and half and one sugar, it occurs to me that he is one of the few people left who actually asks me to do this anachronistic task. Most executives have caught on that Executive Assistants are more than glorified waitresses. Stirring each cup of coffee, I try to remember exactly how many times I have schlepped coffee, accepted undue blame and bolstered a lot of egos for this job. As far as I'm concerned, my dedication has just about reached its limit.

I close my eyes trying to imagine how working in building 99 will be—an airy cubicle, hearing another person's sighs, enduring their idiosyncratic yawns... The years of tireless binder making and lunch reservation finagling begin to weigh on me as I grab the mug handles and walk. Then a happy thought: This opportunity may offer me a chance to glean a few precious nuggets from their furtive conversation.

As I approach, Helen and Mr. Cheroux stop talking. This is typical. Information is never offered to executive assistants in the usual way. That's why I've become an expert at collecting little bits and pieces of verbal exchanges. For the most part I must predict, determine and guess what is happening but occasionally, like with Grace and Karsen, I'll get blindsided.

The rattle of a passing mail cart makes hearing even the odd word impossible as I return to my desk and I distract myself with answering a few emails.

Finally, Helen zips past me and Mr. Cheroux takes the opportunity to grab another cup of coffee out of our kitchen, then slips past me back into his office. He does not look happy. I can't quite interpret what he's thinking, but his body language speaks volumes.

Desperate to find out what is happening with our office and

my job, I opt for the furtive 'mail delivery' approach. Reserved for the end of the day or only in dire circumstances, I pull out a non-urgent solicitation that I hold for precisely occasions like this. It gives me the perfect excuse to check things out in his office or, in this case, gather more information.

His eyes reveal nothing about his thoughts or feelings and he sits comfortably, leaning forward in his office chair. However, every few seconds, he runs both hands through his sand-colored hair. He alternates one hand, then the other, and then both. The result is a slightly tousled look. The casual observer would think nothing of it. In fact, the tousled hair makes him look relaxed and carefree. I have only seen Mr. Cheroux do this a few times, but he is definitely not happy.

I slide the letter into the faux oak "inbox" on his desk and, as luck would have it, he turns his back to me. This offers me an opportunity to quickly glance down at his desk and I see a blueprint with Building 99 circled and Friday's date written in red next to it.

Although I should know better, my curiosity gets the best of me and I attempt an actual conversation. I should amend the list of truths in the assistant world to include: Direct communication never works. It has been my experience at work, that the most important information is never disclosed in a clear, open manner. My attempts at being open and direct have left me verbally battered, frozen out with silence and more in the dark than when I first inquired.

Mr. Cheroux rarely tolerates verbal confirmation of rumors because, as he puts it, he must be notified ahead of time about any concerns so he may have ample time to prepare a response. Before I open my mouth, I can see him bristle. His back stiffens and I clear my throat.

"Um." I say as carefully as I can. "I wonder if you could tell me something about

Helen's visit."

The phone interrupts us and I run back to my desk to pick it up.

"Hello." A saccharine sweet voice oozes on the other end. "I tried Marsha, but she was out, so I'm finally getting to you."

My stomach churns, and I exhale an, "Uh huh."

This most efficient, sickeningly sweet voice belongs to Lana, assistant to Lance's protégé. She slept her way into her current position, starting with the mailroom. At first, I was fooled by her lovely phone manner. Then, I got shot between the eyes by one of her, now legendary, emails.

It all started with her appointment to the position as Second Assistant. Normally, a "Second" would have been relegated to taking orders and pouring coffee. However, an unfortunate mishap with the first assistant, Sam, left Lana in charge. No one is completely sure how he could have contracted e-Coli as a vegetarian, but Lana took over in the blink of an eye.

Within minutes, she was at my door looking our office up and down. Upon my asking if she needed help, she officiously, sniffed that she needed to immediately know the location of her boss' next meeting. After receiving a confirmation that our office was, indeed, the correct location, she began a litany of requirements to be done upon her boss' arrival. Coffee should have two and a half creamers—never two, blinds should be shut because the glare is way to harsh for her boss' eyes and finally— this is the one that still gets me, I should only address him by his surname.

The game-changer happened after I began to set a meeting with four studio heads, my boss, Marsha's boss (who's also my boss' boss) and Lana's boss (the underling.) Usually, underlings let others do the planning and just say "yes that date works." Not so with Lana. She saw an opportunity and essentially took over the meeting plan. I think she used the word "tag team."

Laughing, I said that I had planned thousands of meetings myself and would be fine on my own. The next thing I knew, I received an email copying all the studio head assistants as well as

Marsha and I. Here's what it said:

Dear all,

Because Marsha heads up our little team here, let's make sure we leave the planning to her. After all, without an organizational hierarchy, we'd have chaos. Thanks so much,
Sarah, for all your help. You're an awesome
support person! We'll take over
from here. Thanks! Lana

Okay. For those of you who don't understand the subtleties of email decorum, Lana pulled a rotten one by thanking me for supporting her. It makes it seem like I'm the underling and, of course, there is that incredibly irksome term, "tag team" which means, "I'm going to take over the project, make your work look like mine and act like you were never a part of it."

Needless to say, whenever I hear Lana's voice, I grit my teeth. This time is no different.

As Lana prattles on about scheduling and her boss' requirements, I picture the blueprints on Mr. Cheroux's desk. I know those offices in building 99. The executives have a comfortable space and the assistants have to share an open room, which is divided into cubicles.
Suddenly, I notice that Lana has stopped talking, then she snips, "Well?"

I have absolutely no idea what Lana has said and, therefore, no answer for her. "Lana, you know that your boss reports to my boss, right?"
Silence. Then Lana stammers. "Whh...what?"

"You heard me." My voice begins to shake, but I continue, "Your tone makes it seem the other way around, but your boss reports to mine. Remember that the next time you need to know the exact location of the coffee urn in relation to your boss' seat at the conference table!"

"I...I don't know what you are talking about. I stood up for you when Marsha called and asked how I thought you were doing. I'm not a trouble maker!"

I slam the phone down hard. Looks like my trivet of truth will be more elusive than I first thought.

That evening, I get some comfy clothes on, light some candles and wave sage around my living room and kitchen area. I learned this from a friend I met in a personal growth seminar masked as a "clarity session." Sage clears the negativity and I could use some peace.

Next, I kneel down on a pillow.

Today was tough, Mary. I'm being downgraded. My unwritten "lot wide" résumé...a big red down arrow..."tag team"...Maybe my dad was right and I really am crazy...

Dissolving into a heap on the floor, tears streaming down my face, I imagine I am that small speck of dust, invisible to everyone. Then, wiping my tears and pulling myself up, I ring the Tibetan bells three times and sit back on my heels. Above me on the wall is an enormous portrait of Mary Tyler Moore.

Why Mary Tyler Moore? I learned a long time ago, that the road to sanity is often not paved—or marked, for that matter. In times of trouble, Mary has seen me through.

Then I smile to myself. At least I still have my parking spot.

CHAPTER TWO – GREET THE DAY

Not bothering to brush my teeth. I just gather myself up and crawl over to bed.

The next morning, I get up late and rush to get dressed and out the door. By some miracle, I make it into the office only fifteen minutes late. Mr. Cheroux is on a panel at a conference. He always turns his cell phone off and won't be back until after lunch. That doesn't remove the invisible tether connecting me to my phone and computer.

My backside barely hits the seat when, almost on cue, the phone rings. My heart sinks as I look at the caller ID.

"I tried you earlier." Lana's tone grates in my ear. "Thought maybe you decided to take the day off." Then with mock concern, she continues, "Is this job getting to be too much for you?"

Out of the myriad of choices of responses, I opt for silence.

She needs more details. Can she get the exact number of turkey sandwiches ordered for today's staff lunch? Her boss prefers turkey and she's taken an informal poll and three others enjoy turkey as well.

I tell her five. That should be more than enough in a room of eight people, and quickly hang up before she can ask another inane question.

The phone rings.

"Hi Sarah. Bruce is setting up a conference call and I'm trying to coordinate with your side. How's 3pm?"

"Sure. No problem, Grace."

Hanging up, I begin to type the meeting into the calendar when the phone rings again...
"Hi. It's Marsha. Ken needs to see Lance at 3."

"Well...I've just set a meeting with Mark and Lance is out at a conference so I can't check..."
"Make it happen, Sarah." Click.

A shudder runs through my body and I shift my gaze to our fully appointed office and I try to take my mind off of the gnawing feeling that Grace and Karsen have been gossiping about me. Who else knows?

Hands shaking, breath coming in short heaves, I do my best to calm myself by turning my attention to the move. How in the world are we going to pack everything we've accumulated over three years in two days? I look at my tidy desk with its ample storage space, pick up the phone and wearily dial.
"Hi Grace. Can't do 3. How's 4?"

"We have to do it at 3." Grace's voice tightens.

"Well, we can't."

"Alright, let me get back to you." She's annoyed.

This type of interaction is the staple of my day. The accouterments have eased my pain and discomfort—until now.

Unsettled, I gaze longingly into our private kitchen. We have a full-size refrigerator; sink with hot and cold filtered water dispenser, a toaster oven and cabinet full of any type of beverage imaginable. The coffee maker bubbles and belches in a chaotic rhythm—sounding like Karsen and Grace in a taunting chant. *You're crazy, Sarah...Crazy...Craaaaazy. We all know. We all know. You're crazy Sarah... Craaaaazy.*
We all know. We all know. Craaaaazy... Panic pulsates through my body.

Oh, God, what if I really am crazy. Within seconds, I'm having trouble breathing and put my head in between my legs so I don't faint.

"Sarah Marks' parking spot has been revoked."

I whip my head upright and catch the back of Stan Krokowski, the Head of Grounds Services, talking on his mobile phone outside my door. Put simply, he has the power to giveth and taketh away parking spots at will. His will be done.

"She needs to move her car by tomorrow morning, Security will remove her on- lot parking sticker and apply the new, Green Lot sticker Friday morning. No, I don't know where her office is, never met her before in my life. I was just meeting with Helen and I'm sure she'll say something."

Blood rushes back into my head and I try to retain my equilibrium from having my head upside down.

The Green Lot was where I parked when I first arrived as a temp on the lot eight years ago. It is so far away, that I wore several pairs of heels out before I got smart and started wearing tennis shoes and carrying a backpack. It sucked. For the first few days I had permanent parking with my job, I floated up to my office. The parking spot alone removed about twenty minutes from my commute. Why, besides the obvious wear and tear on shoes and commute change, does parking or moving office matter so much?

Imagine you have to fly to Hong Kong from LA. You get to the airport and the flight attendant at the gate says she is going to upgrade you to First Class. You've flown to Hong Kong for years but have never spent the 14 and a half hour flight in first class so, although intriguing; you have no reference point to gauge an opinion. You know you'll never be able to afford a first class ticket on your own, so this is a treat—a one-time event.

The flight is amazing—hot towels, French wine, luxurious seats that fully recline and are separated by a drape for privacy. But, luxury has its price. As you disembark, you realize that, unless another fluke occurs, you will not be flying to Hong Kong via First Class any time soon.

This lack becomes an obsession. Where there was no desire either way in your mind, now you have a vacuous space —echoing and empty—an aching desire, which lingers for an indefinite period of time.

That is what being an Executive Assistant is like. You could stay in your First

Class job for years (I've known some that have gone over thirty years without a disturbance) or, just when you've gotten comfortable, the job could end and you'll be back at square one.

Which, I realize, is exactly where I am as I quickly poke my head out into the hallway and watch Stan's fat backside round the corner out of sight.

At lunch, I take a walk to clear my head. The outdoor mall is crowded with people and I make a beeline for the food court, praying all the way that I do not run into anyone I know. Thoughts of how to get out of my predicament whirl around my head. For the first time today, I actually start to think of a positive spin on my situation. At least, I reason, I'll be away from all that gossip. Then…

"Oh my GOD!" the Crabtree and Evelyn salesperson steps back into the store and yells something to her coworker. I keep walking. These days I really can't get excited about anything, let alone someone else's drama. It is now noon and the California sun offers no mercy as I attempt to dodge its all-illuminating spotlight. This weather is a stark contrast to the dreary freezing February winters of my childhood in Kansas City. I'm really not hungry. But I continue walking and wishing myself to another universe. WHY are people looking at me? Not that I'm not cute, but really, how rude of people to outright gawk. Just then I look down and BAM.

I'm wearing two different shoes—two completely different types and colors of shoe—one brown loafer and one black pump. With a deep breath, I turn on my two inch black pump heel and walk right into Talbot's, a store from which I never would buy anything, let alone shoes, but desperate times ... they are a woven light brown flat. In my defense, the previous choice of shoes did have the same height of heel. After my face-saving purchase, I shove my mismatches into a bag and stride out into the searing sunlight. The comments and stares follow me all the way back to my office.

I relive each moment of my experience in glorious, horrifying detail and even go into the back-story of the Crabtree and Evelyn salesperson's life. I imagine the shop worker's mocking look, the Talbot's salesperson's quiet contempt. What brought her up to the moment just before she saw an idiot woman with mismatched shoes?

When I arrive at my apartment, I immediately decide to go to bed. Even though its 7pm, the room and most importantly the neighbors are uncharacteristically quiet. I pad across the small space past my TV and into my bathroom. Another positive thought: at least I don't have a studio apartment.

Washing my face, I look deep into my blue-green eyes. All I see are crow's-feet, deep crevices between my brows, bags and dark circles ... ugh. Squeezing my eyes tight, I try to imagine a more improved, less desperate version of myself. Pop! Sadly, I'm still the same person – only this time with more lines and creases from the intense eye scrunching.

I snatch a small tube from a product-filled shelf under my medicine cabinet. The tube reads: intense eye improvement. Lifting my blue and white bedspread, pink woven cotton blanket, purple flowered top sheet, I climb in bed, wondering if the eye cream company makes an all over body cream.

Friday morning...crap...crap...what a stupid day. I have spilled coffee all over my gearshift. My perfectly prepared French Press Pot French Roast drips down my hand and onto the sleeve of my butter yellow blazer. I'm also late for work... again...of all days to be late. That's okay, because what do I really do all day? Making coffee for other people and smiling has never been an aspiration of mine. And yet, here I am. Making bitter drip coffee (or is it bitterly making drip coffee) and pasting on a horrible pleasant demeanor that makes me want to go into my boss's private bathroom and vomit. I'd better put that on my list of things to do before the day is up. No more private bathroom.

When I arrive at the studio, I park, then move quickly upstairs where, praying to remain unnoticed, I slip into my office and begin the task of packing up. The first items to go into boxes are the files. Using a marker, I write "Building 99" on the left side of each banker's box. I create a sort of rhythm as I hold one handle and punch my fist inside the box to flatten the bottom. Then, laying the box on its side, I shove as many files in as possible before shoving top flap A into slot B.

Mr. Cheroux does not show up all morning and he has nothing on his calendar, so

I continue to pack in this oddly comforting manner until lunch. As I fold the last box in Mr. Cheroux's office, I do a once over and discover several papers have fallen behind his credenza. Since most of his papers had been piled there, it makes sense that a few would slip between the wall and the furniture. I slip my hand in and manage to grab all three by the corners with the tips of my fingers.

Two of the pieces end up being ratings sheets, however the third piques my interest. It is a packing slip dated three years ago. The company name listed in Trebacon. Well, I hadn't thought of this spelling. There is no address or number and the only information, besides the name is a P.O. number.

Folding the paper in half, I walk out to my desk and shove the packing slip into my purse. As I stand, I come face to face with Lana. She must have snuck in while I had my head down in concentration.

"Hi." She shows her teeth.

I barely say, "Hello," and continue to shove binders into an already full box.

She eyes my desk and then edges toward Lance's door.

"Can I help you?" I dust myself off and walk toward her, protective of my boss' privacy.

Then she walks into the pantry and places her hand on the counter. "Just checking it all out," She says with a maddening wink.

Vultures! I make sure to lock everything up tight before walking to lunch.

The studio commissary is crowded and I decide to take my turkey on rye back to my office. This will be the last time I'll be able to savor the view and luxuriate in my luscious privacy. As I sit at my desk, I breathe in the peace, the calm, the utter aloneness. Rays of sun shoot through my boss' door and illuminate small particles of dust, which hover and sparkle in the still air. These particles are invisible until the harsh light is shone on them. The sun's rays just miss the edge of my "Make It Count" coffee mug and cut a swath through the room like a laser beam dividing my past and future lives. The creamy maple drawers and cabinets glow in the morning sun and the decor bursts with importance and grandiosity through its minimalism.

I didn't choose the furnishings, they came with the job. For years, I reveled in this crisply decorated office and its impersonal aloofness. Within these maple parameters, I've created a safety-zone, a world in which I am uniquely titled and qualified to participate, despite the harsh competitiveness of my co-workers. In my buffered space, I am blissfully alone and protected against the intimate corporate insensitivities of daily work life. A tightness grips my chest as I relive my hallway encounter with Grace and Karsen and wonder if the information has made it's way around the lot. It is, after all, an extremely small place.

Lance Cheroux was the youngest man in studio history to have the title of EVP. He was initially hired as a consultant at the age of 25 and was promoted with lightening speed to EVP. He has won awards, produced many plays and films and, most important, has attained the pinnacle of power in any studio. He has a front row center parking spot located directly across from the Executive Building. This speaks volumes about the confidence the studio heads have in Mr. Cheroux's abilities. I have worked for him for about three years, an incredibly long time in the studio assistant system.

As I take a bite of my sandwich, I hear a rattle and catch a glimpse of Mr. Cheroux whizzing past my desk. He slams his door loudly. A trail of alcohol gently curls around my head and seeps into my nostrils.

Luckily, I've packed most of Mr. Cheroux's office because he does not come out for the rest of the day. Nor does he take any calls. Not that there have been many calls to take. It's almost like everyone got a simultaneous email announcing the undocumented but highly visible downward slip of Lance Cheroux and his loquacious assistant.

Before I leave, I tiptoe to Mr. Cheroux's door and press my ear to it. Nothing. No movement, sighs, not even a cough make its way through the thick wood door. I take one last look around and sit in my car, holding on to my parking spot for an hour listening to
National Public Radio.

CHAPTER THREE – FIND TOOLS THAT WORK

The next morning, Saturday, I wake up and lie looking at my ceiling in a blissful state. Then I remember my impending office move and my stomach begins to churn. I decide to let the office move go, at least until Monday.

It's almost afternoon so I make some soup. That's a healthy lunch. As I pour the can of chicken noodle into the pot, I see an unopened bag of vinegar and salt potato chips through the half opened cabinet above the stove. I pour the heated soup into a bowl and while it cools, decide to have a few chips. I finish the soup and the entire family sized bag of chips. As I dip my fingers into the bottom of the bag to get the last bits of "vinegar and salt goodness" I remember the many downgrades over my illustrious career.

I spend the rest of the day in my apartment, blinds closed from the searing, sunny day outside, eating my way through my kitchen, ending the day with the stale candy from last year's Halloween party. The sweet chocolate is eaten out of necessity, of course, to balance out my previous salty binge. As I lie in bed that night, I silently give up on myself or ever making anything of my career. I turn out the light and fall into a dreamless sleep.

On Sunday, I sit in front of my television trying not to think about who will be my cubicle neighbor. Bored with the Coach rerun I've been ignoring, I take a look around my apartment. It seemed like a palace the first time I saw it. But after a year of living with this small apartment, I feel cramped and quite intimate with my non-friend neighbor. I know more about this woman than I do about some of my closest friends. She yawns loudly right after her alarm goes off each morning. And, she gargles to the tune of "When the Saints Go Marching In" every evening. A few months ago, I awoke to her boyfriend (or bedmate) yelling at her. Just as I was about to judge the rudeness of the hour, I looked at my nightstand clock and it was 10:00 am! I was late and so was everyone else in my building, maybe even my street. There'd been a blackout.

I used to live with a girl. Jill. We met on the set of a movie on which I was working as an extra. My first year in Los Angeles was spent on television or movie sets working as a "background" or an "extra." What this means is sitting around for countless hours waiting for your turn to be on camera. Being an extra is all about the "bumps," which are little pay raises of $40 to $100 dollars. A bump can be awarded for a special piece of 'business' like walking across a room or even nudity, although I never did the latter. Background work proved to be the perfect way to get to know my new city of residence and the studio system. During my stint as an extra, I was on a television shoot and got called over to the producers. They told me I might get a bump but they needed me to stand in front of them and turn around. I couldn't see any harm in this because there were both men and women there. What could they possibly want me to do? I turned and they all nodded. I would, the producers agreed, get the "bump." When my turn came, the director came over and told me to stand at the camera, then walk to a buffet table several yards away and get some food. That seemed simple enough. So, the director called action and I did my bit. As I stopped at the table, I heard the dialogue. Apparently, one of the characters had a video camera at this party scene and was caught by his wife taking close-ups of my ass! Great. My first big bit and it's my ass that everyone is going to see. There goes the call to mom and the friends in Kansas. A gorgeous woman with shoulder length, curly, dark hair came up to me afterwards and introduced herself as Jill Snell. After it was over and I gathered my things to leave, Jill told me she had overheard the producers talking about the scene earlier in the day. Why hadn't she said anything? My ass was more entertaining, she said, than the television shoot. This was followed by a request for a date, and foolishly, my entertaining ass and I accepted.

Jill continued to have fun at my expense throughout our relationship. I finally ended it when I found out she had gone to a strip club on several occasions, which was something I had told her, many times before, really bothered me. It's been about a year and we are sort of friends. I think about her from time to time. Occasionally, she shows up. Usually, it's a booty call—okay, it's always a booty call.

I get a piece of paper out of the kitchen drawer and write:

I am Stuck

I need to lose weight

I need a better me

I hate myself for being stuck

I give myself no credit

I have many ideas that go nowhere

I am stuck

As I read over my list/poem I notice my newly purchased shoes over in the corner. I consider throwing them in the trash but my good Midwestern upbringing wouldn't permit such a transgression. "Perfectly good shoes" is what my Grandma would say. I replay the previous week's shoe catastrophe again in my mind trying to come up with a reason for this ridiculous behavior. Why … WHY … WHY! Back to the list/poem and being stuck. It's no mystery that I am stuck, but what can I do, that can make any kind of difference? I have pages of list/poems and goals and meditations. Other people seem to get through the day without any major issue. Why do I have such a hard time? Back to the paper— I write:

The kids used to laugh at me during recess. The games they played were about dodging balls and kicking balls. I was a pacifist. Then the hate note came. "No one likes you. Why don't you just go away?" So I did. Now I'm an adult. Work is tough (nothing like school). A memo comes past my desk: Your work performance does not meet with the standards of this company ... Blah, blah, blah ... I want to leave. My girlfriend doesn't like Italian food. My dentist is too nosy. My girlfriend gossips about the wrong people.
I want to leave.

I leave.

I leave.

I leave.

I left. I
left. I
left.
The mail brings an invitation "Please come to our wedding." Oh
my Lord

– commit to a specific date. What if I want to leave? What if I'm
trapped?

I'll suffocate. Best friend's wedding or TV at home? Weigh the two. Hmmm. Difficult decision. Then there's a knock at the door: Girlfriend, with Italian food. The phone rings: Dentist has moved to a psychotherapist's office (she can vent there). I get a card from my girlfriend: Did you know John Travolta has a hairpiece? Okay, no acceptance and acknowledgement overload. Hmmm. My writing sucks.
The end.

I decide to go to bed. Things will be much clearer in the morning.

Monday morning. I fight for one of the last parking spaces at the far end of the Green lot. And, since I couldn't bring myself to wear sneakers, I have the beginning of two blisters on the back of each heel.

The office and its offending cubicle are as small, cramped and communal as I remember from temping. When I stand, I look out over a landscape of beige aluminum and fabric, peppered with pictures of children and dogs and cutout cartoons. My cube shares a wall with another, three connected cubes are across a narrow, industrial carpeted walkway. All occupants are busy at work.

Surrounding this cubical core are the glass front executive offices, brightly lit box seats to the daily entertainment business floorshow. As I sit in the stained, remnant desk chair left behind, I'm haunted by images of all the desperate souls who inhabited this confining space.

Mr. Cheroux enters with his usual flourish—with no trace of desperation and

throws a, "Hi," over his shoulder.

The only person Mr. Cheroux calls by himself, is his wife. I've learned from previously overheard calls, that he is trying to find his wife's niece, a recent college graduate, a job. He continues:

"No. It hasn't been that long, Liz. She can't just wait for other people to tell her what to do, that's what secretaries do."

Not much of our routine changes in the new space. Only now, I have to walk into the community kitchen to get coffee and avoid the combo stench of the day—old Spaghetti-O's, copy machine toner and snoozy-time mint tea— and so does Mr. Cheroux.

"Sarah?" Kimber Colt's sweet voice catches me mid-pour. We worked together during my first few years as a temp.

"Hi Kimber." I try to sound upbeat.

"So…Karsen told me you were coming back."

Great, just what I need. A Business Class mole.

"Yes, we're here now." I keep my voice even.

Kimber walks me out and gives me a quick tour. "Everyone here works on the film side. My desk is over there." She points to the three adjacent cubicles. Kimber's is the furthest away from mine. "Dunphy is next. He's the IT person for our area."

Dunphy is in his mid-twenties, has earbuds in place and is oblivious to our exchange.

"And then Helga. Hey Helga, this is Sarah." A petite, older woman looks up from her typing, waves and goes back to work. Kimber lowers her voice, "Almost retired." Then louder, "That's Mo." Kimber points to the cube directly behind mine. The woman has a blonde buzz cut and John Lennon glasses and is on the phone and typing.
Kimber whispers, "Lesbian."

Back at my sticky desk—it's up to me to wipe down my keyboard, desk and phone to remove the previous occupant's soda and afternoon crumbs, I sit poised and ready. I choose to believe that these are the only ingredients in the pervasive tacky layer as I scrub off my desk. Let the calls begin.

Nothing.

The surrounding hive of cubicles is abuzz with activity, but Mr. Cheroux's office—and therefore my cube are completely silent.

After the third cubicle wipe-down, the phone finally rings. It's Marsha.

"Lance, please."

"Um, Marsha?"

"I want to speak with Lance." She's never used my first name, but this is a new low. "Now."

I don't respond. Instead, I walk into Mr. Cheroux's office and inform him of the

call.

Slipping back into my cube, I hear: "Busy office. I'm Mo."

Although I'm not in the mood for pleasantries, I manage to say, "I'm Sarah." Pulling out the top desk drawer, I notice the previous owner(s) have left me a little gift, crumbs. There is no way to pull the drawer out and empty it into the trashcan, so I use water and a paper towel to dig the little suckers out. As I turn to get another paper towel out of a moving box, Helga, the impending retiree, gives me a jolt.
"Oh," I say, "Hello. Didn't see you there."

"Glad to see you're settling into my little office space." She points to a conference room behind my cube. "I've got one conference room that fits twenty and another just down the hall that can fit ten," She leans in and whispers like she's sharing a deep dark secret, "but it's a tight squeeze. A lot of executives use it for their most confidential meetings because it's so private." Then she straightens up and says loudly, "Let me know if you need anything. I'm just over there."

It's strange to hear someone take such personal ownership of an office, but, I figure, everyone has her way of working and, in the cramped space, maybe Helga's world is this office space. To each her own.

Mr. Cheroux calls me back into his office.

"Marsha wants you to go to her office to pick something up."

"What is it?" I ask suspiciously.

"I don't know." He no longer seems desperate, just slightly annoyed.

"Say 'hi' to Marsha for me." Kimber's soft voice follows me out the door. "Sure.

No problem." I yell back just before the door closes.

I limp outside, heels grating, pupils fighting to adjust to the natural light. The breeze, sun and fresh air make me want to crawl into a hole. On the upside, I'm outside— somewhere I rarely went even while in my previous building.

I pass by our old office. It's empty, except for a phone repair guy kneeling on the

floor. Shaking my head, I skulk past Grace and Karsen's doors. If they see me, they don't respond.

Marsha makes me wait. I stand in front of her desk as she haughtily taps at her keyboard. I can't see her monitor. But, whatever she's doing looks exceptionally important. Without even a glance in my direction, she grabs a binder and hands it to me. "I need five copies."

The binder is not only thick, but also crammed with dividers.

"You know we have a copy shop."

"Yes. And I need this now."

"I'll take it over to the copy shop."

"The copier in our building is quite efficient. The copy shop can't get to the work until tomorrow and I need this today." Then, as an afterthought, "Also, I need that small conference room for Friday at 3pm. Please book that room for two hours and arrange for coffee service and a fruit plate." With that, Marsha returns to her mysterious, yet all important, work. So many things I could say run through my mind: I don't work for you, Marsha. Who the hell are you to tell me what to do! Shove it, Marsh!!!

Instead, I take my shoes off and use the back stairs up to

the copy room. I also notice, as I skim through the binder, that every other page is double sided.

CHAPTER FOUR – BASE YOUR BELIEFS IN REALITY

Day Two in my cubicle captivity. Trudging up from the green lot—I got the last spot in the back—gives me the sensation of having two hot pokers digging into my shoulder blades. My purse strap digs into my clavicle and my backpack bounces off of my neck in a jarring rhythm. I'm late, I'm late, I'm late, I'm late …

I can see the message light blinking as I round the corner into my cube. Hitting the speaker button, I dial my voice mail, fling my purse into a file drawer and sit heavily on the matted office chair. This chair feels like it has been pressed lifeless by many a desperate buttock. I miss my old chair with its mesh, breathable bottom.

There are two messages. I unlace my sneakers as I listen.

"Sarah. I'm working from home today. Hold my messages until tomorrow."

I relax slightly and pull my heels out of a large canvas tote. Then…

"Hi Sarah. It's Kathleen from Human Resources. We have a new executive starting in your old building. Marsha suggested you as someone to help him out and
Lance said it would be fine. Give me a call and let me know you got this message."

I hit the "drop" button to hang up and stare up at the white, faux-cork ceiling. "Last job I had ended the same way." Mo's interjected opine is met with a cacophony of

comments. "I'd quit if I were you."
"Me, too."

"Don't do it. You can't afford to be out of work, Sarah."

"Yes she can. She's has an IRA."

"I don't think she'll get it."

"No she won't."

"How the hell do you know?"

"Because she's got anger issues. No one will take a risk on a rager these days."

"Hey Sarah, I've got a binder I want you to copy…"

The entire group erupts in laughter until I break the silence.

"ENOUGH!" I yell. All activity ceases as I continue my rant, "Who are you people anyway? Why don't you all mind your own business?"

That last sentiment, reminds me that I need to book the conference room in our building for Marsha. The online booking system only allows certain people to book certain rooms. This one has not been updated to allow a building occupant to book, so I call building services and book the room for Friday at 3pm.

Then, I call the commissary and ask for coffee and fruit to be delivered a half hour before. Two tasks done, limitless to go.
"Do you know, when you were little, you told
us you were going to move to

Hollywood?" my grandmother had told me years ago.

I don't remember. All I know is that I hated the Midwest and wanted to do what everyone else did after college. So, I interviewed with the top companies in Kansas City and told them I would relocate to California. The first interviewer asked if I was insane and the second company actually flew me out here, but neither job panned out. After a long, deep depression and a cold Kansas winter, I suddenly realized that I could be this depressed and miserable in another place–say, California. It was amazing that this realization had eluded me for so long, but when it hit, it hit hard. I was gone by March. In fact, it was eight years ago this month that I packed up my black Honda hatchback and moved to Los Angeles. At the time, my parents, friends and everyone around not only thought I was crazy but told me so. It's okay. They have no idea what they are missing. I really enjoy my life in LA.

If only I didn't get caught up in this survival of the sycophant carousel. "Believing is achieving" was my mother's motto. She'd come home from work, the smell of public transportation, lipstick and Chanel No. 5 still clinging to her silk blouse. Then, she would change into her purple terry cloth robe and the lesson would begin.

Things used to be different with my mother. I can close my eyes and see myself at ten years old. My mother and I are cuddling (or is it clutching) each other on the couch and watching a rerun of the premiere episode of the Mary Tyler Moore Show. It remains my favorite episode to this day.

We are rapt with the scene unfolding before our weary eyes.

Mary, a Midwestern

girl from a small town, has just moved to Minneapolis, Minnesota. She interviews for a job at WJM, a local television station with a tough newsman, Lou Grant. He presents her with all the questions one legally cannot ask in a job interview.

"How old are you?" he asks.

"Thirty," she answers without hesitation.

"I like that, no hedging."

"Why? H-how old do I look?"

"Thirty."

My mother watches the television with a blank look of desperation and a grimacing smile. It looks as if she has practiced the perfect "look" of serenity and happiness for hours and hours in front of her bathroom mirror. Yet, she has only achieved a faint version of both. I, on the other hand, have done a much better job. I look completely transfixed and transformed – at least for the moment. Mary's discomfort finally outweighs her need to please Mr. Grant and she tells him that her religion, marital status and age are all illegal job interview questions.[i]

"You've got spunk," says Mr. Grant and for a brief moment Mary thinks she may be winning this difficult man over. "I hate spunk!" he spits.[ii]

"Mom." All I have to do is turn my head and my lips almost touch my mother's ear, "Mom, what's spunk?"

Mom is hugging me but is somewhere else. So, I turn my head back to the television. By ten, I was used to being ignored, with or without television.

For the rest of the episode, I watch as Mary struggles against her own need to please others and their need to take advantage of her good nature. In the end, Mary gets the job and after arguing throughout the episode with a brash New Yorker named Rhoda, who insists the apartment is hers–Mary gets a home. Rhoda's only saving grace is that Bess, the little neighbor girl, loves her "Aunt Rhoda." Despite their differences, Mary and Rhoda become best friends. So, she gets a home and a friend. The stage is set for Mary's adventure to begin. An adventure of a lifetime.

My mother turns off the television and I go to my room. I have learned that it is best to stay out of my parents' line of

fire when they are both home at the same time. Tonight, as I sit on my twin bed in my tiny room, I hear an argument starting up and begin to panic. I grab an old magazine of my mother's, with Mary Tyler Moore on the cover, and start to flip through it. But I cannot shut out the now increasing sound of voices and crashing pottery. I close the magazine and stare at Mary's calming smile.
"Please," I say to the serene picture, "I need a rest from this." Just then, the noise stops.

My mother, out of breath, appears in the doorway.

"You're going to your grandmother's place," she says, hurriedly packing my

Barbie suitcase. "Grab your shoes and let's go."

I am elated and a little unsettled by what has just happened. Was it a coincidence?

I decide it wasn't and grab the magazine for safekeeping.

[RRRRRING]

My office phone is ringing and I haven't even noticed.

"This is Sarah."

"What are you wearing?" The voice on the other end annoys and gives me the
creeps at the same time. Too bad I know who the caller is.

"Hi, Em," is all I can muster. My eyes roll toward the ceiling round the drapes and stop on my shoes. My stomach drops.
"Hey, I asked what are …"

"I'm at work, okay?" I snap. This is a "newish" girl I've

been seeing who is perfectly nice, but not at all my type and the only reason I stay with her is because I am nice. Eternally nice. Sickeningly nice. That's why when I started out many years before as a temp I was deemed the girl who could work with the "difficult" people. I really can work with anyone. The bigger the asshole the more qualified I am for the job. That's because, being in the entertainment business takes two types of people— those who are shitty and those who are shit upon. Guess which one I am. Well, I am shitty, but mostly to myself. That doesn't count, right? The upside to my current position is its perks. Mr. Cheroux receives all the Academy movies before the Oscars and he receives another from the distributors. Em works in the DVD distribution center and thus, my movie collection has grown exponentially since I've known her.

As Em drones on, I drift into a day dream/memory, which takes place in my house back home. I'm five years old and sit nestled on the living room couch with my orange and blue crocheted wrap around my long, summer-tanned legs, which are tucked beneath me. My eyes are glued to the television as I mindlessly take popcorn out of a large plastic bowl and carefully put it into my mouth. As I crunch away, I play a little game with myself – if I take my eyes off the flickering screen, then the show I'm watching is not real. But, if I remain loyal, perfectly attentive to the story and characters, then it is gloriously real. I can be transported, at least for a half an hour, into their world, their life and out of my own.

In the background of my life, there is a loud
crash and the tinkling of glass

shattering. The sound of adult voices is heard coming from the next room. The louder they get the closer and more intent I am on the television screen. The argument moves into the very room in which I am sitting. I, by now, have practiced this "TV-portation" and am oblivious to the screaming that is going on right over my small, blonde head.

"Fucker," my mother says and she storms in. Her auburn

hair is a mass of large curlers covered by a plastic hair dryer cap. A long tube, which is meant to attach to the hair-drying base, flops uselessly from the cap.

"Bitch," my father drunkenly follows my mother next to the couch.

Mom has now worked herself into a fury and is red-faced and shaking. The hair dryer tube accents every word as she screams, "I am sick of this shit. You have fucking abused me for too long ..."

Distracted by the flailing tube and listing to the left in an attempt to stand erect, my father spits impotently. "Abuse? You've got the crazy family . . ."

Before he finishes, my mother clenches her fists, punches the air and screams "I can't take this anymore."

My father lowers his prematurely salt and pepper head and hisses, "If you leave, I swear to God I will make sure you never get custody of Sarah. I'll tell the courts about your crazy mother and your hysterical, fucking fits. You will NEVER see her again.
Never."

My mother stands, stunned.

I have heard the words coming out of my father's mouth and although I don't dare take my eyes off the television, I well up and try to make myself invisible. Pulling the covers up under my chin, I pretend to be as small as a speck of dust on my blanket. Dust doesn't feel anything.

My mother absent-mindedly puts her hand on my blonde curly halo of hair, but I have succeeded in becoming like dust and I don't feel it.

My father is long gone, having stumbled out of the room to unceremoniously plop himself on the bed and light a cigarette—all bloodshot eyes, bleary and cold. He mutters under his flammable breath, "Fucking, crazy bitch."

I bury myself into the scene on TV. The Mary Tyler Moore

Show's main character, Mary Richards is upset with everyone in her office because they've been cracking jokes about the recent death of a dear friend and co-worker, Chuckles the Clown. For the entire episode, Mary chastises her friends as they make fun and titter with laughter at the circumstances of his untimely end. He was crushed by an elephant while dressed as a peanut. They are all now seated at the funeral and the minister speaks of Chuckles the Clown's warmth and generosity.

Mary's friends are solemn as the minister recounts a particularly cherished story about this man who lost his life so suddenly. Seated on the aisle, in the midst of all the grieving family and friends, Mary begins to shake uncontrollably. Her friends look back at her in surprise – was that a giggle? Mary momentarily calms herself and the minister continues with another anecdote. A loud "HA" escapes Mary's lips and the whole room looks at her, including the minister. He stops the eulogy and points her out and says this is how Chuckles would have wanted to be remembered. For the laughter and fun he shared with everyone he encountered. As the entire group stares, the minister encourages her to let out the laughter she's been trying to suppress – there is a long pause as Mary looks around her and the group waits for her reaction. She takes a deep breath and bursts into a heap of sobs and tears.[iii]

I flip the TV off and sit silent and alone. My mother is in the kitchen making a cup of tea. I listen intently to make sure both parents are out of earshot and softly sing to myself "Happy Birthday to me, Happy Birthday to me, Happy Birthday dear Sarah,

Happy Birthday to me."

"Sarah, Sarah, SARAH?" I awaken from my daydream to Em repeating my name.

She has asked me a question that I have yet to answer.

Suddenly I realize what I need to do. "I've got to go, Em." I hang up the phone and sit in silence. It's pretty quiet because my boss is away. Mr. Cheroux is away from the office all day—no explanation given and, honestly, none asked. I'm happy to have my own time. No noise except for the occasional loud yawn from Mo, my cubicle mate.

I grab a piece of paper and write:

What Would Mary Do?

I sit for a while just looking at the paper. This is how I'm going to live my life from now on.

CHAPTER FIVE – THE FILE

The Saturday morning sun streams into my apartment and onto the large picture of Mary Tyler Moore. I do a double take. She's smiling serenely and yet at a certain angle, there is a subversive look lurking behind the tranquility. An unsettled shiver runs through me as I light a candle and some sage. On my "shrine" I place a small heart shaped rock that I found on a hike in the Santa Monica Mountains. Then I ring the bells three times.

Where do you think she is, Mary? It's been almost a year and she hasn't called or emailed. Mom's always been distant, but you'd think she would at least check in and let me know she's okay. Actually, it's probably better off this way. We were never very good at talking.

I go over to the kitchen cupboard and grab five macaroons then quickly eat them in succession. Pop...chew, chew. Pop...chew. Pop...chew, chew. Pop...chew...chew... I look at the last one and exhale. Pop. I chew as quickly as I can.

Putting the kettle on, I take some French Roast beans and put them in the coffee grinder my mother gave me before I left Kansas City. Carefully taking the French Press Pot apart and methodically cleaning it with soapy water, I rinse each piece even more thoroughly. I have learned that this meticulous attention to detail pays off in maximum flavor. My coffee is better than any coffee house's I've visited. I press the grinder and inhale the warm scent. This is my favorite smell in the whole world–comforting an invigorating. I love the smell of ground coffee even more than the smell of the coffee as it is first poured in the morning. That comes in at a close second. I put nine slightly rounded teaspoons of ground coffee in the French

Press. While I wait for the kettle to boil, I go to my purse and take out a crinkled piece of paper. On it is written "What Would Mary Do?

I write:

No GOSSIP.

See REALITY for what it is.

Look for the BRIGHT SIDE in that reality.

Find INSPIRATION in unlikely places.

Take ACTION based on previous information.

The kettle whistles madly and I turn off the gas stove to let the water cool ever so slightly. One must never pour boiling water over coffee. I wait three minutes and then gently pour the water onto the back of a spoon and into the French Press. So, what is reality, anyway? Something we make up and use to rationalize our actions? Writing these five steps inspires me. Stirring the coffee water mixture I put the press into the glass carafe, without pushing it down, and breathe in the warm generous aroma curling out of the carafe.

I carry everything, including the "Star" mug that a KC friend, Greg, brought me a few years back, over to my desk and glance at the clock. I must wait exactly five minutes to push the plunger down and pour the coffee. Any more time will make the coffee bitter and any less will make it just a little too thin. As I take a moment to look around my little apartment I try to remember all the people who have stayed on my hand-me-down pullout couch—dubbed "the bed from hell" by one unhappy guest. My estimate is about twenty or so friends have slept in torment for a night or two. Most of the visitors have been pretty impressed with what I've accomplished so far. On the piece of paper, under "See REALITY for what it is" I write:

INTELLIGENT

ATTRACTIVE

UNDERACHIEVING

WAY TOO NICE

STUPID

I stop and cross that word out. I shouldn't be so hard on myself. But I'm such an easy target. Instead I write:

WELL MEANING BUT CHALLENGED IN THE WAYS OF THE

WORLD

It's time. I push the plunger down on the French Press and pour it into the mug.

As I sip and enjoy the fabulous cup of coffee I've created, it occurs to me that I'm not entirely objective. I write:

OPEN TO NEW IDEAS

That's what I need right now. If I'm going to learn something about myself, I should ask a trusted, Rhoda-like friend. Unfortunately, there is no one in my life that comes close. I have good friends, but they are all far away. Anyone in close physical proximity could care less about my issues with women or my preference for fantasy films. Most of the people I've have met, especially lately, are self-absorbed and flakey. Come on, surely there is someone who knows me well. The only people who know me are back in Kansas City. Those are wonderful friends who, apart from thinking I'm insane, also care about me. They may have utterly no idea what it is like to work in an industry where the location of lunch has as much, if not more, importance than the lunch meeting itself. But my friends love me, just the same. It took me a year to realize that I must memorize the hippest trendiest restaurants for my boss's lunches.

I write:

CREATIVE

I was once fired for sending a man I was temping for to the same restaurant three times in a row. Part of an assistant's job description at a studio should read 'must stay current with new clothing styles, new restaurants and new trends, so that you can discuss pertinent information with clients, create dynamic lunch venues and buy memorable
Christmas gifts.'

When you are in your early twenties, it's so easy to make friends. It seems like people flowed in and out of my life pretty easily back then. After living in LA for almost ten years, I have found that most people have their friends. And if they don't, they are serial offenders. Part of it could be my fault. I'm just not as malleable as I used to be.

I write:

STUCK

Sitting back, I look at the list. My requirements have gotten more sophisticated and my tastes have changed.

I see that my file cabinet is open and start to shut it, but because it's so full, it won't budge. Opening it, I discover the culprit, my overflowing purge file. Should I dare look at it? When I first moved to LA, I was alone and bored. To combat the ennui, I would go to coffee houses around town and spew my "just moved to LA" crap onto paper. I am shocked at the volume of paper that has accumulated over the years and I leaf through the carefully labeled "Purge File."

My favorite movie is "It's a Wonderful Life." Fantasy in every form is my genre. Leaving the emotional heavy lifting for another time, I escape to my car and drive to the movie theater. What's so bad about a fantasy to take my mind off of real life? The air conditioning feels heavenly as I stand in the popcorn line and look down at my too tight jeans. I never weigh myself, but judging from the tightness of my clothes, I could lose a few pounds. I deserve popcorn and put on extra butter flavor just to cement the fact. The double feature is called "Double Fantasy." The movies are "Xanadu" and "The Wizard of Oz." At the intermission, I grab some chocolate almonds, my favorite. Screw the "Purge

File."

CHAPTER SIX – THE BRIGHT SIDE OF REALITY

Monday morning. Fifteen minutes early, I manage to snag front row parking and try to make a noiseless entry and slip into my flattened, stained office chair. The same pervasive silence greets me as I attend to my daily email and voice mail checking. Even
Mo stays mum.

Suddenly, a voice booms from the entrance.

"SARAH. Sarah Marks!"

I slowly stand up and peer over my cube wall to see a mop of white hair bounding through the fabric Habitrail maze. Before I can step out to greet this man, a hand juts toward me. I know Mr.

Barlow. Well, I know of him. His name has been in every trade magazine since I came to

Los Angeles. He's won five academy awards and countless Emmy's for executive producing blockbuster movies and hit television shows. Pretty much anything he touches, turns to gold.

"Brink Barlow. Marsha said you were the one who set up Friday's meeting. I was next door at another meeting and wanted to thank you, in person."

In all of my time as an executive assistant, I have never been thanked for setting up a meeting in a conference room, let alone in person.

I force words like "nice to meet you" and "well, I'm glad you did" before he nods and is off on the whirlwind, from whence he came.

Lowering myself onto my greasy chair and shaking my head, I, try to catch my equilibrium. Wow, kindness, I didn't expect that one.

I go about my business without a thought until I notice something odd. Silence. Usually, the activity and noise level borders on distracting, but everything seems to have gone deafeningly quiet.

Then, I hear the whisper. It is the same tone Helga used in explaining in intimate detail that the small conference room can sometimes squeeze in ten people. I can just make out Kimber's voice and the word "Sarah" floats through. Training my keen sense of hearing toward their conversation I barely catch the words "unstable" and "doesn't know her place." But, it's no use. A delivery truck idling outside creates just enough vibration to block out anything else.

As I get my morning coffee from the communal kitchen, Kimber and Dunphy cut their conversation short. They quickly change the subject.

"Your detective work paid off, Dun." Kimber says brightly. "Looks like that information I was looking for was exactly where I thought it would be."

"My pleasure," Dunphy shoves his earbuds in and pads out the door.

It's not worth the effort to ask, "What the hell is going on?" or "Were you two just talking about me?" They'll only deny that their conversation has anything to do with me. Plus, I have no proof.

Back at my desk, Mr. Cheroux remains silent, as does the rest of the group. I decide the best tactic is to ignore them all— rise above it, so to speak.

"K. Sarah Marks." Kimber's voice hovers over my desk.

My stomach drops. What on earth is happening? The only place I'm listed with my first initial is on my social security card and the conference booking website. Then Dunphy chimes in, "What's the "K" stand for, Sarah?"

If I ignore them, they will continue taunting me. But, if I don't, they'll probably do the same.

I opt for a quick response, "Kimberly."

Mo speaks to me for the first time today. "Did you ever call Kathleen from HR

back?"

I can't see anyone, but my stomach churns and I wish myself anywhere but here.

What could I possibly have done to deserve this?

Then I realize, Helga is at her desk and has said nothing.

To confirm my suspicions that she has systematically turned the entire group against me, I decide to walk past Helga's desk. Sure enough, she will not even look at me as I pass by and her eyes shift nervously from computer to phone, then back again.

The rest of my day is spent recalculating my daily budget and searching for other executive assistant positions. Life is way too short.

It is still light when I get home and the weather is hot and uncharacteristically humid on this June day in Los Angeles. I have no air conditioning in my small apartment and have opened all the windows to create a meager cross breeze. A neighbor's television blares downstairs. I stand in front of the file cabinet. Avoiding my "Purge File" has absorbed my every waking hour. Finally, I can't take it any more. I turn off the "I Love

Lucy" rerun and grab the file aggressively. A couple of pages fall out and I retrieve them.

Following the "no accident" rule of life that my therapist taught me, I read these stories first. There is no date on any of the stories, but I guess they must have been written a few months after I arrived in LA. Before I read the first piece, I carefully light some sage and a few candles and ring the bell on the Mary altar.

Here we go, Mary. I get the feeling this will lead to something. Maybe that elusive trivet of truth. Well, wish me luck!

I go over to the sofa and settle in with my first story:

> When I was a little girl, I would sit for hours and wait. I would think to myself, boy, this (whatever the event happened to be at the time) is taking so long, but I'll just wait for a few more minutes. I'd wait for anyone; friends, family... all they would have to say was "wait here" and I would. I have kept that habit.

> When I wait, I mostly sit and write or watch people or even tell myself "one more minute, then I'm leaving." But for some reason, the minutes turn into hours. I've been known to wait for people for up to three hours. That comes from my innate ability to not miss a single event that goes on anywhere.

> When I was little, my grandfather called me "How Come Havarti" because I asked so many questions. I never wanted to go to sleep for fear of missing what was going to happen next. My family used to have to trick me. They would all pretend to go upstairs to bed in single file, so I would follow them. I was so gullible. You know, come to think of it, there was

a time when I believed anything. What am I saying, I still believe anything. One hot summer in Florida, I was three at the time. My family was traveling to the beach when I spotted an amusement park. Being the inquisitive child I was, I started with my usual battery of questions.

"Is that a Ferris Wheel? Can we go see it? How tall do you think it is?" Finally, my cousin Freddy who was used to this and seized every opportunity to ridicule me said, "Oh, you thought that was real? That's a moving billboard."

I bit. "A moving billboard?" I asked.

"Yes, that is just a picture of rides moving around, but they're not real." They still talk about that incident to this day. Things like that follow you around. Especially, in a family situation, you fall into roles. Once branded, I became the family questioner and, of course, the butt of every gullibility test there was. So maybe that's why when people start to tell me that they are studying to be a rocket scientist and I say when will you graduate, it seems very natural to me. I'll always be the same smiling little girl believing that there are such things as aliens who abduct people and have children with them, or that when the refrigerator opens, there are little men who march in formation to turn on and off the light.

I close my eyes. A memory seeps into my mind's eye. It is so vivid I open my eyes to make sure I'm in my apartment. I sit back on my couch and close them again. I'm twenty. I am sitting on the stoop of my childhood apartment building and when I look down, I can see traces of an outline of a snail's trail all shimmery and slimy. I also try to conjure any happy feeling. Anything at all, was there ever an ice cream induced euphoria, a puppy...my thoughts are interrupted by my mother's huffing. She is carrying a large box brimming with hats as she exits our apartment building. She finds her keys, unlocks the car door (all with box still teetering in one hand) and uses a foot to pry the driver side door ajar. Amazingly, all the hats stay in the box as she shoves it far into the shallow back seat of her dirty blue hatch back. I chuckle to myself. My mother's purse is more organized than this car–and that is not saying much. The small car is filled to capacity.

And my mother goes back and practically sits on the hatch to close it.

"Okay," my mother seems resolved, set, almost stony as she approaches, then hugs me. Abruptly, she walks back to the car and turns just before she gets in "You're fine. You've always been fine."

She looks at my face, red and distorted from held back tears. "Look," she sighs unmoving. "You've got a job and I've left you in good hands. Bob is very dependable." Then, as she gets in the car, rolls down the window and adds, "You're fine."

I watch the worn car chug away, get up and numbly walk into the building. The unlocked door stands slightly ajar and I take my time walking into the apartment. The place seems so much bigger without my mother's presence. It is stifling inside. The empty unmoving air enters my lungs and pokes giant holes every time I breathe. I walk from room to room, ending up in the den. At least she left the couch and bed. I plop down on the sofa. There is a sharp pain behind my right eye and nothing takes it away, not even my palms pressed hard against my eyes. I feel a familiar brush on my leg and peek around my palm from my left eye at Bob, my golden retriever.

"She says you're dependable, Bob."

Then the tears come. They are unstoppable. In all the years I spent alone with my mother nothing prepared me for this.

[WHOOOOSH]

No one looks up as I pass by, the next morning. My entry into cubeland is
frighteningly seamless. The silence is palpable.

It's almost impossible to take. I can't decide whether having everyone talking at once is better or worse than having total silence—except the occasional whisper.
Kathleen from HR has not called again and Mr. Cheroux's calls have all but stopped. Perhaps this is all for the best, this respite from work has given me a chance to further hone my listening skills. I make it through the day by counting the times I hear the word "protocol" whispered from Helga's cube—32.

Back at home, I nestle into my precious privacy. The weather has cooled a bit, so I open the window and as I make my way to the couch, a piece of paper under my foot crinkles. Leaning down to pick it up, I see that it's another piece of the unending puzzle.
My "purge file" story.

I smelled the jet fuel as the plane took off. It reminded me of when I was a little girl and I used to fly to see my grandparents. Even then, I knew it was to escape some terrible thing that my father was going to do. I was escaping. The flight attendants used to take me by the hand and I'd feel butterflies in my stomach. But I was a brave little girl as I stepped onto the big airplane with its airplane fuel smells and the combination of smoke, perfume and closed-in cabin.

I was three at the time, but whenever I'd smell airplane fuel, I would know I'd be going away soon, escaping to the arms of Grandma and Grandpa. One little girl in pre-school named Laura, before such a trip, told me that she hoped my plane crashed and that I died, too. I remember looking at her and thinking she should have to go in my place for saying that. But I was the one dressed in my plaid kilt and red cardigan sweater being led to that ominous runway.

The flight attendant would take my hand and lead me to that funny feeling I would get just as the plane would take off. The entire plane would shake and I would hear such horrible noise I was certain we were going to crash, just as Laura said. Then, just as suddenly as the noise was there it was gone and the plane was completely peaceful. The pilot would give me wings after the flight was over and then I would victoriously be led away from the huge machine that brought me there. For at least another moment, I was safe and sound. The smell of jet fuel lingered on my clothes, only to be washed off during my bath that evening.

[GULP]

Oh, what the hell. "Why am I taking my time with this stupid purge file?" I pick a random page and read.

My father was a drunk. He used to stumble into the room with the smell of stale smoke and liquor deep in his clothes and incoherently try to have a conversation with my mother. I remember this in two ways, a jovial happy go lucky guy who "goes with the flow" or a screaming maniac who considers no one but himself.

I was only three at the time, but I remember many things about that man.

He used to take me to bars during his visitation when I was a bit older, like
five years old. The bartenders used to give me cocktail sausages and talk to me as if I really belonged there; even then I knew I didn't. But I'd sit and wait for my father to drink a few with his buddies and then drive me back to his apartment where he'd make me Ovaltine. I remember there not being much to do there.

Those memories of him screaming and falling still rage on in my mind, especially recently. I'm filled with shame. I think it's all the shame that he should have had, plus quite a bit of mine thrown in, too. So whenever I drink, all I can see is a man who cares about no one and has no conscience. I think my mother used to say the "no conscience" thing a lot.

Anyway, from that time on, I have fought to get rid of those things inside of me. But whenever my mother or I saw a movie or a play or television show with someone who was drunk, we would be rattled for weeks. I always wondered if he realized how much he tortured me.
So years later, when we had regained contact, I told him about the bars and memories of drunkenness and all of the hurt he had caused me. He didn't say a word. No apology, no excuse, nothing. Later, though, he did start to make rationalizations about the situation. He only took me to one bar and was it such a big deal? Well, I asked myself, how big of a deal was it? I look in the mirror at the seemingly calm and normal woman in front of me and all I really

see is a frightened ashamed (I still don't know of what) little girl. So, I say, what difference did it make that my father was never there? What was the big deal about a man making a child's life a living hell? That my so-called "father" drank so much? For years later I felt relieved to just have peace in the house, and to this day if anyone has a drunken experience near me, I am deeply, deeply effected. How much of a difference? How much?

My hands shake as I type the hand written words into the computer. Each word makes me catch my breath and a few times I stop, stand up and stretch. It's almost like the writing is coming through my body.

Seven – Find Inspiration in Unlikely Places

Who knows how many mornings I've made the Green Lot trek? The days blend together in a horrendous montage of nasty looks, furtive glances and inside jokes, none of to which, I am privy. Vowing to stay true to my agreement to abstain from gossip, I continue to overhear tidbits from this small group's gossipy whispers. So far, I've surmised that Helga will not give up her malevolent, passive-aggressive activity until I holler "uncle." What she has underestimated, however, is that I have dealt with the best of malevolent passive-aggression way before she came along.

Until, that is, I encounter a whole different level of crazy. Lately, I've been eating outside in the picnic area and today, as I nibble my Havarti and avocado on rye, I am startled by a voice behind me.

"Hey, Sarah." Helga stands with tray in hand, smiling as if nothing has ever happened between us.

Surprised, but cautious, I nod and slightly smile. "Hi."

"May I?" She begins to sit.

"Um, sure."

"What kind of sandwich is that?" Helga shows absolutely no trace of the malevolence I've experienced for well over a week—or is it two, I've stopped counting.

"Looks like you're settling in just fine." Helga picks at her small green salad., chases a cherry tomato round and round, then moves on to an easier to pierce piece of jicama.

"Yes." I wonder what she is up to.

"Brink Barlow certainly likes you." Helga jabs her fork into the tomato with force.

"He called me..." Then, I stop. Why am I explaining myself? I feel her jealousy and anger, but that is not my fault.

"Look, Helga. I get that you're angry about my booking the conference room…and well, you need to stop talking about me."

She cuts me off, "I have no idea what you are talking about. You're one of my favorite people. Why, just the other day, I was telling Kimber what an efficient person you are…" Those shifty eyes again. Helga puts her fork down. "I feel sick. I might have to go home, I feel so bad. I am not a gossip."

"Well, then. I guess, we're done here." There is, obviously, no reasoning with

Helga so, I excuse myself and go back to my desk.

Unsure of what to expect as I reenter the tomb of terror —as I've begun to call my cube cave—I answer a few emails and double check some appointments.

Slowly, the office begins to fill up and, much to my surprise the noise level rises to when I first moved. Guessing that whatever it was must have blown over, I continue with my tasks.

Mr. Cheroux's line rings and Brink Barlow is calling.

"Hi, Mr. Barlow. Just one moment for Mr. Cheroux."

"Wait." Mr. Barlow's tone is both jovial and professional. "I need to call upon your expertise, once again, Sarah."

"Okay." I reply tentatively and almost feel Helga bristle.

"Would you mind booking the same conference room for a meeting tomorrow at nine a.m.?"

"Okay. How many people will attend? Would you like coffee and pastries?"

"Four and just coffee. I need to keep my fabulous figure."

We both laugh at this and right after we hang up, I book the conference room and order the coffee.

A pall envelopes the office, the likes of which can only be equated with the moments of green-gray sky, seconds before a tornado hits. It is then that I see precisely how fraught with insecurity Helga is and to what lengths she will go, to push the waning boundaries of her job. As I pass by her desk, she nervously shifts in her chair, picks up a few sheets of paper, shuffles them, and then replaces them in the same spot.

Silence, once again, sweeps through the office. This time, however, there is no whispering. No frantic flurry of hushed conversations to piece together.

Instead, my phone rings. Stomach drops. Lone straw snaps.

"Hi, Sarah!" Lana's voice literally squeaks with jubilation.

"Building Services says you have the conference room in your building for tomorrow at nine and I need it. Can you please move your meeting elsewhere?

"This isn't for Mr. Cheroux, Lana. It's actually for a high-level, off-lot talent."

Lana's tone verges on screechy. "May I know who it is?"

"Sorry, it's confidential." I'm annoyed but satisfied that I finally have a trump card in our little card game.

After hanging up, I can't help but smile to myself. In the back of my mind, I realize that Helga has not spoken a word at her desk, nor has anyone else in our office. But, this is the first time in weeks that I feel like chuckling, so I push any suspicions aside. Whatever she's got, I can take.

It's 7:00pm and Mr. Cheroux's packing up to go home. I take the cue and am about to shut down my computer when an email pops up on my desktop.

Hi Sarah!

I just got off the phone with Brink Barlow's office and they say it's fine if the meeting is moved to a more suitable location. I took the liberty of calling the commissary and building services to let them know of the change. I also let them know that, since I'm in the Executive Building, I can do any further booking for their office.

Thanks!

Lana

The only way Lana could have known that the conference room was booked for Brink Barlow, was through someone in cubeland. Slowly, I rise out of my chair and peek over my cubical wall at Helga. She appears to be hard at work, moving a stack of reports from one side of her desk to the other, lips pursed, watery eyes jerking from computer to phone to waste basket.

The next day, during lunch, I risk my parking spot to meet with a temp agency. Sometimes there is no parking upon return from lunch and the only option is finding parking off the lot, which means about a mile walk to building 99. I decide it is worth the trouble. It's anyone's guess how much longer I'll be able to take this torture.

I choose a small agency, SmartOne where no one knows me. I could have chosen a number of large and well-known agencies, but all I want is to remain invisible and make some money. I am surprised by the reception when I arrive at SmartOne's offices. I hand my resume to a heavyset man in a cubicle. His name is José and as he reads, he eats a glazed donut. Crumbs fall all over my resume, which has been carefully printed, on linen paper.

José bounces out of his ergonomically correct chair and yells back, "I want you to meet Gary."

Gary is the co-owner of SmartOne. He brings a certain "air" to the office and not metaphorically speaking. He has the worst body odor I've ever smelled. I hold my breath and inhale with my head turned to the left. During my few minutes in the chair across from him, I've found a small fresh air pocket is located there.

"Well," Gary exhales as he talks.

His breath causes me to recoil even more than I did when I thought of signing up for this work.

"You've got quite a resume, Sarah. Lance Cheroux, 100 words per minute, you've got so many software suites here I'm amazed. Are you looking for permanent work?"

"Not really. I'd rather stay open for other opportunities." *"Please God. I want to*

be anywhere else but here doing anything else but this." I think. But I keep my pleasant, calm and professional demeanor, all the while, in my head, throwing up, jumping up and down and screaming at the top of my lungs. I cough a bit and add a little prayer that the interview will end soon.

"Okay, you're all set. Talk to José on your way out and he'll set you up." Gary stands up and shakes my hand.

I grab my bag, and as I open the door, gasp for breath. I feel like a diver coming up after a fifty-foot free dive. Gulp. Gulp…Ahhh. I find the bathroom and thoroughly wash my hands. I would prefer to take a shower. Was this man really that disgusting or do I really hate temping that much?

Back at my desk, I take a big bite of my turkey on wheat and the phone

rings.

Chewing quickly, I manage to say, "Hmm…Hmmlo."

"Hi, Sarah. It sounds like I might have caught you at a bad time." It's Brink

Barlow.

"Mmmm…no." I hold the phone away from my mouth as I chew. "Just having a

little lunch."

"Sarah, I just signed a contract with KRG and would like to hire you as my assistant in

Los Angeles." Then quickly, "I've got Bree in NY, so you'd work with her."

"Your assi….?" Realizing

that the entire office is, most likely, listening, I cut
myself off. I can almost feel everyone's ears prick up upon
hearing my tone.

"Yes, I've already contacted your HR rep, Kathleen and
she is fine with it. Since I'm a do-it-yourself guy, I wanted to
call myself and offer you the job. What do you think?"

"Yes. I'd love to. Thanks so much." My mind is whirling.
Usually, Executive announcements like this don't slip past me. I
must have been so preoccupied, the news went right by. Come to
think of it, I would usually overhear this type of news in the
Executive Building halls.

"That's great, Sarah." Mr. Barlow says warmly. "Oh, no need to
worry about Mr.

Cheroux, I've spoken with him and he is fine with our
arrangement. Okay. So, I'll see you Monday morning. Kathleen
said she would email you with the details."

"Okay. Thanks. Yes...Monday." I hang up. Me? Back in the
Executive Building?

Although I hear or see no one in my office, I can feel the group's
attention trained on me.

Dunphy, one earbud pulled out, Mo staring intently at her
computer screen, Helga and

Kimber breathless—all straining to hear and know the latest
piece of information.

CHAPTER EIGHT – MOMENT OF CLARITY

That night in bed, the day's events whirl around in my head. As I drift off, a memory seeps in as a dream.

The plane is crowded and I settle in. Hanging bag overhead–check. Backpack under seat in front of me–check. Crossword puzzle–check. I'm wedged between two men. One tidy office type and the other a working class Joe type with a trucker's cap, and yes, a toothpick. When I first sit down, I imagine that I'll speak with the tidy office gentleman first, but working class man starts up a conversation.

"You know, this is a great responsibility," he says.

I look up from my crossword, pen perched above my lap. "Oh, yes. The exit row does have certain requirements." I look back down at the squares on the crossword.

The man looks out the window. Crap, I've been rude.

"Uh, I was visiting my mother in Kansas City. Do you live there?"

"No, I'm from Oklahoma but my daughter just had the first grandbaby in our family. A little girl." The plane begins to taxi down the runway picking up speed. "What's her name?"

"Kimberly Sarah Williams." He sits up a bit taller as he says this.

The plane is now in the air and going through clouds. Behind the man's trucker cap there is a sea of gray, then the plane breaks into the blue sky and I can see large puffy, white, mountains of clouds. *Bump, bump.* I look down at my crossword, ugh, turbulence. *BING.* The flight attendant asks everyone to remain seated. A flightless bird, I read. *Bump, bump.* E – M … *BING. Bump, bump, bumpity, bump.* The flight attendant says they will delay beverage service. U, I continue. *Bump, bump, BANG.* My breath quickens. It's only turbulence. I sneak a look at both men. Each looks fine. I'm okay.

Bump, Rattle, a rat a, RAT A TAT TAT … BANG!

Okay, that was scary. I grip my pen and begin to silently pray. The only prayer I can think of is the Lord's Prayer. Our father who art in heaven … *Rattle, Rattle, RATTLE, RATTLE, BAM* … my crossword, pen, along with someone's popcorn and several drinks fly up in the air, AAAAHHHHH, the chorus of voices yell like they are all on a roller coaster as the plane plummets. Then regains–all is calm. I am hyperventilating, my eyes are squeezed shut, and my fingers are gripping the armrest. In all of my years of flying, I have never experienced anything like this or been this terrified. Then, I feel something rough on my hand and I realize that the working class man has put his hand on top of mine.

"Sarah," he says. "What does your daddy do?" "Huh?" I open my eyes and look at the man. "You told me about your mama, but what does your daddy do?" I am still breathing hard and anticipating another sudden drop, but am nonetheless touched. I close my eyes and the words are out of my mouth before I can even think.

"My father was a drunk. He used to take me to bars when

I was a child. He left when I was five, and even when he had visitation rights, he didn't use them ... He didn't choose me. He didn't choose me ..." I softly weep as this stranger calmly looks at me. This stranger's hand holds more comfort than I got in my entire relationship with my father.

"Well," the man says simply, "I do believe if you were my child, I would try to move heaven and earth till I got to see you. There wouldn't be nothing to keep me from seeing my baby."

With my free hand, I wipe my eyes with my sleeve and say, "I'm sorry, I've forgotten your name."

"Sam."

"Thank you, Sam."

It wasn't anything I did that made my father behave like a shithead, it was his

choice. And the fact that he didn't choose me makes me angry–extremely angry. He is a person. The fact that this total stranger has done more for than me in a few minutes, than my father did for me in our lifetime together is tragic. Even sadder, is I've spent that time believing that I could do something to change who my father is or how he behaves. My father may not have chosen me, but I can choose me. I CAN CHOOSE ME!!!

Sam holds my hand as we silently ride the smaller bumps, as the pilot apologizes and as the flight attendants check to see if everyone is okay. After we de-plane, I turn to Sam and give him a quick, chaste hug. Sam nods at me kindly, picks up his bag and blends into the sea of humanity.

Friday morning, I awake at sunrise and the reality of my new Senior Executive

Assistant position sinks in.

Suddenly, I have an overwhelming desire to contact my father. This piece of good news sparks a feeling I haven't experienced since I was a child. Funny how I still have his entry in my handwritten address book after all these years. I read each number and letter carefully and run my fingers over the smooth area. It is written neatly, and unlike some other entries in the book, my father's entry has no bumpy scratch-outs. As inconsistent as my father is, he has been in the same house since he left. Since he is on the East Coast, it's not too early to call.

Looking at the phone, I try to conjure the words. What will I say to him? "Sorry, dad." No. "I forgive you, do you forgive me?" Yes. That's what I'll say.

Picking up the phone and dialing, I get a recording on the other end, "The number you have dialed has been disconnected or is no longer in service..." I must have misdialed. I redial the number carefully checking the address book entry. I get the same recording and a bad feeling begins to form in the pit of my stomach. My father hasn't moved in fifteen years.

I go to my computer and do a search–Bryant Edward Marks–and stare at the monitor in shock. The top link reads:
Obituaries – Bryant Edward Marks, Indiana

I click the link and read:

Bryant Edward Marks – Died last Thursday, June 18th after an extended

illness. He is survived by his wife, Lena Kramer Marks and their daughter, Mickey Lynn Marks. Donations should be sent to the Pulmonary Institute, 10704 E. Second Street, Gary, IN.

A single tear slips down my right cheek and I quickly whisk it away with the back of my hand. This cannot be happening. I re-read the obituary twelve times and then turn the computer off. I missed my father by a month.

I close my eyes and try to remember my father's face and see him as clear as day.

He is smiling and grimacing as he shakes his best friend's ten-year-old son's hand. His favorite trick is to pretend that young children have incredibly strong grips. He occasionally falls to his knees. Not in this case, though. Instead, he looks over and sees me walk up his driveway, nods to me and his face completely changes. Another tear, this one on my left cheek is ignored and is joined by a gasping hiccup. I have only experienced this feeling once before and it was when I realized my father really wasn't coming back to live with my mother and I. Now, I remember my father's face. We haven't spoken for two years and our parting was not pleasant. When I first moved to LA, he had offered me some money. Feeling I deserved restitution after all those years without child support, I decided to take the monthly stipend of a few hundred dollars a month. A few months into this agreement, he began to pry into my life and challenge the way I spent the money. One day, I had enough and told him I didn't need a father…now. I wasn't five any more. He said, "Okay" and we haven't spoken since.

I fall to the floor, right next to the Mary shrine and sob. My face is pressed against the taupe pile carpeting and my tears drop onto the Scotch Guarded material and disappear down deep into the carpet's backing. Briefly, I think about what those tears must be meeting deep down in a place I've never seen. I'm not sure if I'm crying for him, me, or the lack of either.

Pulling myself up onto my knees, I face the Mary shrine. "Hey Dad, I saw the obituary. Did the woman and your daughter know about mom and me? Were you sick when we last talked? It says "extended illness" but I don't know how long that means.
Listen, I was going to say this when I called, but … I found out you were… um …"

It's impossible to finish this sentence so I simply say, "I forgive you. Do you forgive me?"

I close my eyes and try to imagine my dad giving me the embrace and answers I never got before. In my mind's eye, I see my father hugging me. A warm glowing and purifying light surrounds us.

Then something odd happens–my father begins to giggle.

Not the mean spirited chortle he used to have, but a genuine, honest giggle that becomes a huge belly laugh. He grabs my hands and starts to dance and spin with me all around. In my mind, I start to laugh and spin, too.

My father says, "I forgive you." Then he's gone in a flash of light and I am alone. I feel calm as I open my eyes, rise and go into the bedroom to prepare for my final day in a cubicle.

It's Friday and the numbness of my morning discovery still lingers. So much so,

that I barely notice my long Green lot walk. Monday will bring a new parking spot, fresh, clean desk and phone and blessed privacy. The reality is still sinking in that as the Senior Executive Assistant to Brink Barlow, I will be two levels over Marsha and countless levels above all of my cube mates.

If anyone knows about my corporate catapult, they don't let on. Then again, I'm too busy packing and readying myself for the next week. Mr. Cheroux doesn't even look at me as he skulks into his office and shuts the door.

A Moment of
Clarity by Sarah
Marks

I had a moment of clarity it
came between episodes of
M*A*S*H and I Love Lucy.
I don't know what
channel it was I only
know I was watching
with the noise of my
mind whirring and the
television on to drown it
out. I was struck with the
clearest and most open
moment I've ever had.
Suddenly, I understood

everything and didn't
worry that I hadn't done
laundry in two weeks or
couldn't pay my phone
bill.
In that moment I could breathe fully, deeply and
without fear.

As I watched Lucy, I knew some cosmic window was
opened to my soul.

Then I thought - What if this ends?

And I knew it was over.

My cosmic window had slammed shut and I was left
to wonder

Will it ever open again?

Luckily, most of my boxes are still packed. Kathleen
instructed me to leave Mr. Cheroux's items the way they are and
to just take care of myself.

"Being moved again, Sarah?" Mo pokes her head
completely into my cube giving me a jolt.
"Uh, yes." I wrap my "Make it Count" mug in newspaper. "I
have a new job."

Invisible ears perk up all over the office.

"Really?"

Standing and dusting my hands off, I look out over the
cubes and say loudly,

"Actually, I've been hired to work for Brink Barlow."

"That's great, Sarah." Mo says flatly. "Knock yourself out."

After packing the final box, I take a break. Leaning back in my chair, I close my eyes and think of the Mary Tyler Moore episode when Mary's ex-fiancé, Bill, comes to Minneapolis to win her back. After two years of living with her fiancé, Bill, he tells Mary that he needs more time. Mary decides to move to the big city and lands a job as associate-producer for WJM. Rhoda, the woman who wants her apartment has moved upstairs.

During her first day at work, Mary gets a phone call from Bill and she invites him over that evening.

That same night, Mary's ex-fiancé hands her a bouquet of flowers. She sees the card and much to his protests, reads it.

"Best wishes for a speedy recovery." She looks at him and realizes that he is still the same.

He professes his love for her and she tells him, "It's funny. I never noticed how you don't say that very well."

By this time Mary realizes that she needs to let Bill go and tells him so.

"Take care of yourself," Bill says.

"I think I just did."

Office services lets me borrow a golf cart to transport my boxes to my car. Before I take off, I walk back in to do a once over in my cube—certainly don't want to leave anything behind here.

I receive and upward nod from Mo, a handshake from Dunphy, a hug from

Kimber and a wobbly, half-hearted, "Congratulations," from Helga.

CHAPTER NINE – BREAKING THROUGH THE DOUBT

The Santa Monica beach is peppered with a few umbrellas and blankets on this gorgeous Saturday. I always enjoy coming to this beach because it is a bit harder to get to than the others. I have driven up the Pacific Coast Highway with my windows down and the cool breeze blowing in; I make a U-turn well past the other beaches and then park on the side of the road. This beach is a little too far for most people to walk to and most people want to be close to restaurants and parking. I hike down the rocks and take off my shoes. The coarse sand feels warm on the surface but cool just underneath, as I walk. It is five o'clock and most people are winding up their beach day. This is my favorite thing to do in the summer.

As I walk to the water's edge, I see two blonde boys playing in the water with their mother sitting on a towel close by. The surf is relatively calm and the boys are splashing and playing. I wonder if my father was ever able to find peace while he was alive. I feel a pang as I think of his new daughter. Did he scream in front of her, throw drunken fits and pass out until well after three every weekend? Or was he a better, more improved version of himself with this new girl. Did he give the new daughter the things he could never give me?

"Mommy, look!" one little boy in the distance yells excitedly. "Look at the crabs!

"There aren't crabs," says the other boy.

"Yes, there are." the mother says with surprise, "Look down. Stop walking and look carefully at the ground."

It's almost like this woman's words are for me. I stop walking and look down. At first glance, I see only rocks, sand and seaweed. Then I see them. The ground is alive beneath my feet. Small crabs below me, all crawling in the same direction I'd been walking. Then I see even smaller crabs going at a slower pace. They are all dragging their shells behind them and making a huge effort to move around rocks and seaweed.

The more I relax and focus my attention on the ground, the more life and movement I see all around me. I crouch and watch this newly discovered universe below me. I see one crab carrying some food and another tiny crab trying to scale a rock, which is more like a mountain to its tiny legs. I turn to say something to the boys and their mother, but they are halfway to their car.

I am alone on this stretch of beach. How many opportunities have I missed over the years by not focusing? Maybe I based my life on what I know, but I have been missing some really, really good parts. And because I don't know they exist, these opportunities have been breezing past me like strangers at an airport.

"Do I want to be the observer or the observed?" I say aloud.

I smile a little, take a deep breath and sing: "Who can take the world on with her smile? Who can take a nothing day and suddenly make it all seem worthwhile? Well, it's you girl and you should know it. With each glance and every little movement you show it..."

I smile more broadly and spin with my head back and my eyes closed. I imagine the opening credits of the Mary Tyler Moore Show during which Mary walks through the city, shops for groceries and enjoys life as a free, independent single woman.

"Love is all around no need to waste it. You can have a town why don't you take it. You're gonna make it after all."[iv]

I laugh out loud as I remember Mary taking off her

beret and tossing it into the air. The song ends with the beret lingering high above her head. I open my eyes. That's why I love Mary so much. She became an icon at the peak of the women's movement. Because women were searching for equality in every part of their lives during the seventies, the sexes were pitted against each other. One major event occurred when a pompous tennis player named Bobby Riggs challenged a female tennis player, Billie Jean King, to a match. To no one's surprise, Billie beat Bobby by a wide margin and women had a new trump card to play–at least in tennis.

The Mary Tyler Moore Show was more than a television program, it was a social movement and people were hungry to see a single woman who was making it on her own and happy about it. Mary became a paragon for successful women who grew up, conquered and won their freedom in work and life.

How is it that I can remember all the words to The Mary Tyler Moore show theme song and yet cannot remember my own PIN number? I chuckle to myself and walk along the water's edge.

As I head home, the walk to my car seems different. Climbing the rocks, I imagine I am the little crab. Then I try to imagine who might be watching me struggle. It's comforting to think that I'm not alone. I also realize I don't have to watch and control everything. All I have to do is concentrate on me. As I drive with no radio on and watch the world go on around me, I try to imagine that I'm on vacation. My trip home is much more exciting than usual. Instead of feeling jealous and angry with my newly discovered half sibling and her mother, Lena, I start to feel something else. Is it compassion?
Curiosity?

Maybe Lena and her daughter can answer questions I have about my father.

Maybe, even though I can't share my thoughts and feelings with my father, I can with these two people. We do, after all, have something in common.

When I get home, I grab a blank card and envelope from my desk and get my address book out. On the card I write:

Dear Lena,

My name is Sarah. I am not sure if you know who I am, but I am Ed's

daughter. I just found out about my father's death and wanted to send my sincere condolences. I lost contact with my father about eight years ago and unfortunately never was able to meet you or your daughter. I recently experienced some events in my life that allowed me to see things in a very different light. After attempting to call my father and heal things up, I found out he had passed away. If you and your daughter are open to it, I would like to meet you and perhaps we can share our stories about Edward. I hope you and your daughter are well.

Sincerely,

Sarah Marks

I decide to send the card to my father's old address, with hopes that either Lena is still living there or the mail will be forwarded. My heart jumps as I put the card in the outgoing mail slot in my apartment's mailbox. What a long journey this letter has ahead of it. I say a silent prayer that it finds its way. Then I take a leisurely walk around the neighborhood.

Los Angeles is a transient city, but as I walk, I realize I recognize quite a few people. My area is mixed with small unit apartment buildings and post-war bungalows. A young Asian woman brushes her fluffy white dog in the alley next door. With quick strokes, the hair flies in a circle through the air and lands like a blanket on the floor of the alley.

I continue past a man who is always outside his
house fixing his dilapidated Mustang.

He looks up and nods. I say, "Hello."

Groggy from the harsh sun, I sit at a park bench overlooking the ocean. The wind has created little peaks dotting the water all the way to the horizon. Nodding and dozing, I dream of an idyllic walk from my old office to the nearby mall. The stores are packed with people and I move through the crowd quickly, to my unknown destination.

Suddenly, I look down at the man's feet right in front of me. He's wearing two different shoes – a Stan Smith tennis shoe and a hiking boot. Then I notice the woman next to him is wearing a cowboy boot and a red pump. Everyone has on two different shoes!

The next morning. My steamy coffee swirls in a white mug early on a Sunday morning. My adrenaline is pumping, so I decide to go to the park and sit and wait. I'm not sure what I am waiting for, but I breathe in the fresh air and make a humming noise as I let the air out. Pretty soon I get restless and walk over to a fenced in dog area. I never really liked dogs, but why not. I open up my notebook and sit on a bench.

But, before I can write anything, I see a piece of paper half hidden under my bench. On one side it reads:

DOG FOOD

WOMEN'S FITNESS MAG

COFFEE

BEER

BEACH TOWEL

On the other side of the paper it reads:

MAKE MONEY

CREATE HAPPINESS

ENJOY LIFE

I'm in love. I look around for the author, but the park is empty. So, I get up to begin my search. But first, to seek some guidance.

Back at home. Three rings of the bell and Hmmmmmm. I sit at the Mary shrine, put the paper in the offering box, ring the bell again and light some sage.

Dear Mary,

All I want to know is who she is. It has to be a woman and she has to be single. I can feel it. It sounds a bit strange, I know. But, I really need for this person to be real. I need for her to be the kind of person who understands me.

I stare at Mary's picture for a few moments. Then I have the sudden urge to go out for a run. As I sit down to tie my running shoes, I notice a piece of paper stuck under my file cabinet. It must have fallen out a while ago when I was going through the "Purge" file. Wow, two discoveries in one day. Thanks, Mary. It is a poem I wrote for Jill. Ecstasy was a feeling I could never comprehend ...

Ugh. I sit down. This one is going to be painful. Talk about living in a fantasy

world...

...until I met you. I've never wanted to feel the warmth I feel, when I am with you. My security is something I treasured and now share as a part of you.

Sometimes you are so cruel and uncaring –

That is the understatement of the century. I continue:

Sometimes you make me feel so special, like a princess or a queen.

Okay, that's enough. This is disgusting. Not only am I subjecting myself to my horrible poetry, but I've also reminded myself of how fleeting romance is and of the female fickle nature. Great, that's all I need right now. I walk over to the shrine, open up the offering box and pull out the note, ball it up and toss it into the dumpster.

A burst of energy surges through my body and I spring up, slam the door behind me and go for a walk. I pass a lovely, tiny beach cottage and a young woman, feet propped up, sipping a beer and watching television with her German Shepherd, catches my eye.

That would be fun to own a house. Maybe someday, I think to myself.

[HUFF, HUFF, PUFF]

More energy pumps through my veins and I begin to run. What intrigues me about the list I just threw away? Probably another loser that I can rescue—I stop and jog in place at an intersection. Whatever the reason, I'm going to put this thing out of my mind. I decide to run through a shady park away from the traffic. As the light turns green,
I cross the street and jog towards the park's entrance.

CHAPTER TEN – REALITY SUCKS

Brink Barlow's office is four doors down from my old office. It is a corner space with a sweeping view of Bel Air and the Ocean. Looks like they vacated, painted and prepared this office during Mr. Cheroux's and my relocation. It is squeaky clean.

The best part, is the parking. My spot is right next to Mr. Barlow's.

As I place my purse in the bottom drawer and unpack a bag of essential items, I turn on my computer. My email seems to be connected and I check Mr. Barlow's calendar. He's got five appointments today. Not bad. He doesn't like to pack meetings together. The first meeting is at 10a.m. Jack Rellan.

Stan Krokowski pops his head in, "Hi Sarah. Is this an okay time?"

Looking around, I am surprised at his familiarity. After all, just a few weeks ago, he had a conversation about the removal of my parking spot, as he stood just within earshot of my office, in which he acted as if he didn't know me.

"Everything is fine, Stan. Thanks."

Handing me an envelope, he continues with a smile, "Here is your new badge. We used your old picture. Normally, you'd have to go to Security yourself, but I thought I'd take a moment to welcome you to your new position."

"Thanks."

"I take it you found your parking spot okay, this morning."

Stan's seems nervous.

"If you need anything at all, just give me a call. I'm Stan Krokowski, Head of

Grounds Services."

"Okay. Thanks for stopping by, Stan."

The phone rings and I answer, "Brink Barlow's office."

There is a pause and then, "Where's Bree?" The voice sounds suspicious.

"Excuse me?" I try to sound calm but cannot figure this person out.

"This is Jack. WHERE IS BREE?!"

"Sir, I'm Sarah and ..." he hangs up before I can finish. What the heck do I do with that? I decide to make some coffee.

Pulling my "Make It Count" mug out of my bag, I head into the private kitchen. It is much bigger than the one down the hall and the appliances are brand new. The coffee is piping hot and I hold the mug below my nose to fully absorb the aroma. Taking in the clean white cabinets, granite counter tops and stainless-steel appliances, I make my way back just in time to get the phone.

"Hi, um, this is Bree."

"Hi, Bree."

"Listen, Sarah is it? Brink has a ten o'clock. Can you access the calendar yet?"

"Yes." I take a look at the calendar.

"Jack Rellan may call. He is worried about how to get on the lot." Bree says. "He just called. Asked for you and then hung up when I tried to introduce myself."
"He a worrier, that one." Bree sounds confident.

"I'll get him a "Drive-On" pass and parking in front of our building." I say just as confidently.

She thanks me and we have a quick chat. I learn that she's been with Mr. Barlow for ten years. I tell her that I've been on the lot for about that same amount of time.

The phone interrupts our conversation.

"Mr. Barlow's office." I am feeling a little more settled in now that I'm getting the lay of the land.

"Hi Sarah." It's Mr. Barlow. "I'll be in just before the 10a.m. meeting with Jack Rellan. Would you make sure he has a pass to get on the lot and parking?"

"Sure." I hang up. So far so good.

The day goes smoothly. Mr. Barlow is a low maintenance man who makes his own calls, sets many of his own appointments and, even better, gets his own coffee.

When Jack Rellan comes in, I realize his bark is way worse than his bite.

The best moment of the day, perhaps of the year, comes when Mr. Barlow says he's tried Lana's boss, left a voice mail message and still has not heard back after a couple of hours. Would I mind calling and setting up a meeting?

Would I? HA! Completely forgetting that the default setting when I make a call is my line, I pick up the phone and call Lana's boss' direct number.

"Hi Lana." I keep my tone even, although I feel so happy, right now, I could jump out of my skin. "It's Sarah. Brink Barlow left a voice mail a few hours ago and wanted me to set up a meeting to catch up with your boss.

"Well," Lana says in an uncharacteristically haughty tone, "You can just tell your boss that he will have to wait."

"Um. Okay. Can you at least let him know that Brink Barlow called?" Lana has no idea that this is the new head of the Studio and I decide that it's not up to me to tell her.

I walk into Mr. Barlow's office and tell him exactly what

Lana said, word for

WORD.

My line rings and I run back to my desk to answer. It's Lana's boss. He is so sorry and promises to have a talk with Lana. Can I please apologize and send his call through to Mr. Barlow?

I gladly do so. There is nothing like justice. I imagine Lana squirming in her seat while her beloved boss lectures her on the basics of studio etiquette. Especially, when it comes to superiors.

On the drive home, I am so giddy from the day's new events, I forget the disgusting poem I found about my ex, Jill, and decide to call her. As the phone rings, I rationalize my actions. It would be so nice to share this experience with someone. Maybe we can just have coffee. I wonder if she's with someone. But before I can consider the alternative, she answers.

"Hi. It's Sarah." It has been a few months and I listen to her ramble about the same old stuff that she used to ramble about. On and on about her data security work and the important people she has met.

"Hey, Jill," I can't help but interrupt. "I have to go. I know I called you, but

I'm...uh busy and...yeah...wanted to say 'hi.' That's all, glad you're well."

I go home, pull out the torn and wrinkled paper with 'What Would Mary Do?' written at the top of it and decide to retype the whole thing on the computer.

REALITY

My father was a drunk. However, it was my choice to carry his drunkenness around.

I am an attractive, intelligent woman who lives in a fantasy world because I refused to see my father's drunkenness as an issue and use that fantasy world as a hiding place.

Some things that may get in my way are underachieving, being way too nice and being stuck. My creative outlook and my openness to new ideas could help me through.

I take a look at the finished paragraph. Yes, this does sound like me.

SEE THE BRIGHT SIDE OF REALITY

I am resourceful and don't have to live in a fantasy; I choose to do so. By knowing these two things, I can rise above my problems.

FIND INSPIRATION IN UNLIKELY PLACES

I find inspiration in the ocean and anonymous poetry/lists. I'm not sure what even inspires me about those things, but it's a start.

TAKE ACTION BASED ON PREVIOUS INFORMATION

I find that aside from writing stuff down, I need to just be where I am and who I am. I can choose to do so every day.

There is a bookstore on my way home. I park and breathe in the luscious scent of books as I walk through the entrance, then head toward the self-help section. I scan the bookshelves for anything that might work for me. My eyes stop on a book called *Writing a Vision for Your Life*. I grab it and look at the first page and read:

This book is a place for you to pour out your innermost dreams and desires. To create your ideal vision, you must first look at what in life you want to accomplish. Why are you on this earth?

I slam the book shut. That's it! I need a vision! I put the book back on the shelf and hurry to my car. I need to create an ideal vision that points me to my true path.

On the way home, I make a mental list of my accomplishments during my lifetime. I've worked in restaurants as a waitress and hostess, been a receptionist and an extra and, finally, an assistant. No one ever calls an assistant a secretary anymore. Well, except for Mr. Cheroux. I liken it to terms like waste management expert and water treatment facility. Even in the best of circumstances, I am just another human receptacle for overly inflated personalities to project their anger and frustration upon. Stripped down, my job is part psychologist, nursemaid, handyman and concierge.

It is dizzying for me to think about how many times I subtly kept people away from Lance Cheroux. Mostly, it was when his king-sized ego was injured by his "heartless boss." I always knew when he was overwhelmed because his characteristically neatly combed, sand-colored hair was tousled as he fretfully ran his hands through it, again and again. It is his tragic flaw. He was a hero who needed my help. So, I creatively hid him away until his sulking subsided, and no one was the wiser. Come to think of it, there were many times when I was able to excuse him from certain important meetings with clever stories of big looming deadlines or secret budding projects. Despite all of this, I wonder if he'll be okay. I decide to let the whole Trebacon issue go and focus on the future.

It will be interesting to see how working for Mr. Barlow turns out. He doesn't seem like the majority of C-level studio executives, he's warm and respectful, but, as my grandmother used to say, you never truly know someone until you see them without their collar stays. Translation: I'll reserve judgment about Mr. Barlow and/or Bree until I see them at their most "relaxed."

[BING! – AHA!]

Each day, I settle in more and more. The fact that I'm sitting back in the very building, I'd been pining away about while in cubicle hell, continues to bring me joy. I can only imagine what the group is doing and, honestly, do not a care about it one iota.

I'm far too busy with Brink Barlow. It turns out that he produced an off- Broadway play that became a Broadway play and a hit. From the way he describes his experience it was not fun. Not fun at all. He says it is one of those things that sounds good to everyone else but is a nightmare to live. Now, Mr. Barlow seems genuine and overwhelmed. I do my best to help the overwhelmed part and try wholeheartedly to enjoy the genuine part.

Bree is an interesting one. We've had little chats here and there, and I find that

I'm having difficulty getting into the flow of information. Usually, assistants are copied

on every document for her boss. It's understandable that, in the beginning, I might be left off some distribution lists, however, I'm completing my third week and still find myself in the dark about a lot of meetings and events.

Mr. Barlow splits his time between New York and Los Angeles and I book his travel in and around Los Angeles and Bree does the same with New York. Trouble is, I find that she has not been forthcoming with a couple of key pieces of information. Not only that, I've noticed that she's getting incredibly chummy with my Los Angeles co- workers.

For example, Mr. Barlow forwarded me a request for a group tour from a personal charity. Since I've done many of these, I started doing the normal arrangements. Then, in the midst of my work, I get a call from the Commissary, saying that Bree has booked the private dining room for the group. So, I give her a call.

"Hi Bree. Heard on the news you've got a huge storm coming."

"Hi. Yeah. It's supposed to bring about twelve inches of rain but we're okay, we're on high ground. I hear the Studio is hot and sticky from a friend I just talked to on the lot."

"Oh?" Okay. Slightly creepy. The week before, she told me she talked to Karsen about the conference rooms. I try the soft approach, "Listen, Bree. I thought we agreed to split the responsibilities—you handle New York and I handle Los Angeles."

"Sure. No problem."

We hang up and I feel unsettled. This is the third time in three weeks that I've had to reiterate the boundaries of our jobs. Settling myself by carefully going over Mr. Barlow's contacts, I discover that the

edits I'd worked hard on for the past three weeks, have been completely erased!

A call to IT proves fruitless and my frustration level increases as I find more errors that I corrected and are now reverted to the incorrect state.

The phone rings. Without looking at the caller ID, I pick it up

"This is Sarah."

"Hi Sarah!" The voice on the other end sounds incredibly happy to speak to me and a peek at the caller ID reveals that it's Marsha.

"Hello, Marsha." I am dumbstruck.

"How on earth are you?" She is frighteningly friendly.

All of these words, put together, don't even add up to the amount she spoke to me while I worked for Lance Cheroux. "Fine. And you?"

"I was so glad to see that you got this job. How is it so far?"

These are open-ended questions, meant to stimulate conversation, but I can only remember back to a time when she sneered, snapped and ordered me around. After all that, I find it virtually impossible to say more than a simple sentence to her. "Things are great here, Marsha. Is there something I can help you with?"

"Oh, well," she continues, "Yes. Mr. Barlow asked to meet with my boss so I wanted to set something up."

"Great." I pull up our shared calendar. "How's tomorrow at 2? Does that work for

him?"

"I'll make it work."

We hang up and I cannot believe that is the same person. For years, Marsha was barely civil—it's a stretch to call it that—the transformation is unbelievable.

[MUNCH, MUNCH – UH HUH]

The next day at lunchtime, I run into Helga. Her smile belies her true intentions.

"Hi, Sarah. How is it being in the Executive Building?"

"Hi, Helga. It's going well." Trying to extricate myself, I begin to walk toward the salad bar, but she follows me.

"You were obviously Mr. Barlow's favorite." She grabs a takeout container and starts building her salad. "You know, if you hadn't of moved into my little office, I would have gotten that job."

"Okay, Helga. Bye." I get away as quickly as humanly possible.

That evening, I take advantage of the late summer light, put on my running shoes and walk out the door. Running has become a part of my after work routine. I always walk to warm up. As I turn the corner I begin to run. I vaguely hear someone yelling, but before I can even look I feel a sharp pain on my left buttock. When I look back, I see a large snarling German Shepherd latched on to my left butt cheek. He won't let go.

"GUS!" a blonde in her mid to late thirties runs toward me yelling at the top of her lungs. She grabs the dog and apologizes. Looking at my bloody hand covering my butt, she asks, "Are you hurt?"

"No," I'm crying. Normally, I would be embarrassed, but for some inexplicable reason, I'm not.

"You look pretty shaken up. I'm so sorry. My name is Harper and I think Gus saw you running and decided that you were a perp. He's a retired police dog."

I half smile and start to limp off, but Harper is right behind me. "Let me take him home…and I'll help you to your place. You live far?"

She darts across the busy street, deposits Gus safely in his house, and then runs back to me.

"Here," Harper offers her arm as support. I quietly limp and she chatters all the way home. She must be nervous. For a brief moment, I think of her romantically but put it out of my mind. She is nothing like the type of woman I normally am attracted to. Harper is regular looking. Average height, baggy shorts and a t-shirt mask her stocky build. Her sandy hair just kind of hangs on her head and she seems a little too laid back for my taste.
Her style is, well, no style.

We arrive at my door and I dig in my pocket for the key. Once I have it, Harper takes it and unlocks the door.

"Listen, I was an EMT for a while. I know my dog doesn't have rabies and I promise I'm not a…" she looks down at her cheese block feet, "well, you know. Would you like for me to look at your wound and dress it?" Harper shifts her weight uneasily and for some reason I trust her.

I say, "No, but thank you." And tell her I'll take care of it.

With a thoughtful nod, she walks out apologizing again for her dog "Gus is a good dog, he's just a bit intense. Bye."

I look at the back of my leg and butt. It isn't as bad as I thought. Gus didn't break the skin when he bit me. The blood is from my hand. His tooth probably nicked me as I tried to push him away. There is just a red mark with some bruising on my behind.

I grab some ice out of the freezer, put it in a plastic bag and lie on the couch with

the ice on my bottom. I wake up with a bag full of water (thank goodness for zip bags) and it is already dark. I have no idea what time it is until I see the clock. It's midnight.

Wow, a traumatic experience can really make me sleep. I get up and go into my bedroom. My butt feels okay. It's a little sore but not nearly as uncomfortable as I expected. I brush my teeth and fall into bed. Face first of course.

[YIKES!]

Week four in Mr. Barlow's office and the collar stays are coming off. Bree, is sick and I get a full sense of just how much work Bree has been funneling away from me.

Over the last month, we've had several extended discussions about the office, our personal lives and dating—we are both single. I have gotten a clear sense that Bree is an intense woman who values her power more than anyone I've ever met. She also let it slip that Mr. Barlow's previous assistant at the production offices in Los Angeles was a
"queen bee."

My inference turns out to be correct. She was not about to make the same mistake twice. Trouble is, I am not the other assistant.

What I discover during Bree's sick day, is not only has she been holding back information, she's also been deliberately funneling distribution away from me.

Case in point: That charity group that I scheduled and then Bree went around me to book. Bree essentially has erased me from any part of the process. The only way I find out is because I get a call from the front gate guard.

"Hi. Is this Bree?"

"No."

The clueless guard continues. "I have a group here and they say they're supposed

to meet Bree?"

I shake my head in disbelief. Is she kidding me? "Actually, I'm the contact person, Sarah Marks. Mr. Barlow asked me to arrange the whole itinerary for the group."

"Well, I don't know. They seem pretty adamant that they speak with Bree. Oh, wait someone wants to speak with you."

"Hello," a woman with a Southern accent speaks, "Yes. I've been communicating with Bree in Mr. Barlow's office."

"Hi, this is Sarah Marks. I work for Mr. Barlow and have arranged today's itinerary for your group. My contact for your organization was Stacy."

"Oh yes." The woman continues, "Stacy is my assistant. I've been speaking directly with Bree. Too bad I won't get to meet her and thank her in person for a job well done. She really went the extra mile for us."

"Click.

The next morning, I arrive at work and my head is pounding. I take two ibuprofen with my morning coffee. Logging into my computer, then into our shared calendar, I notice several meetings in Los Angeles that I did not arrange. The most insulting part is that the participants are Grace's boss and Karsen's boss.

Picking up the phone, I decide the direct approach is best. "Hi Grace. Does your boss have a meeting with Mr. Barlow today at 2?"

"Hi Sarah," Grace sounds unapologetic. "He sure does."

"Great." Then as an afterthought, "How was this meeting set? Did Bree call you?"

"Oh," Grace sounds surprised at my question, "I called her."

"Grace. I'm steps away from you and Bree is in New York." My knuckles are white around the receiver. I am so angry.
"Well, she said to call her with any meetings."

"Grace. You can call me to set meetings." Then for emphasis, 'I'm right down the hall."
"Okay." She says, brightly.

The phone rings and I see that it's Bree calling from home.

"Hey," her voice croaks.

"Oh, hey, I didn't recognize your voice." I am relieved that she's back at work so

I can nip this ridiculous behavior in the bud. "You're back."

"Listen, Bree." Trying to stay calm, I attempt to explain my frustration. "There are some meetings that were set here in LA and I knew nothing about them."
"Oh, I know." She says hoarsely, "Grace and Karsen called me and I just put them in.

"They called you at home?"

"No, they called me the evening before I got sick...day before yesterday."

For the thousandth time, I say, "Again, Bree. Let's stay in our own city. It is impossible for me to do my job if I don't have all the information. Just like the tour group. Why were you even planning the event? First, it's in LA and second, Mr. Barlow asked me to do it."

"Not sure how I can help you with that, Sarah. Brink asked me to follow up and that's what I did."

"But you followed up with the executives!" Now I'm pissed. "Do you have any idea how that looks?" Then it occurs to me that she knows exactly how that looks. This bitch is undermining my job.

"That's my job, Sarah." She hangs up and I am absolutely furious.

Mr. Barlow is leaving for New York this evening and I want to make sure I get clear with him about my job duties.

He arrives at a 9:30 a.m. and, after giving him a little time to settle in, I walk into his office.

"Excuse me, Mr. Barlow." I stand in front of his desk, he is seated. "Do you have a minute?"
"Sure, Sarah. Sit down."

"First of all, I'd like to check in to see if you have any concerns about my job performance. Am I doing okay, so far?"
"Sure."

"I'd like to get clear about my duties in this job. Things are getting a little muddied about who does what where and I'd like to get it straight so I can be as efficient at my job as possible."
"Okay."

"I'd like to verify that both my job and duties include Los Angeles.

After all, I am your assistant here in Los Angeles."

His face darkens, then he says, "That's not my area. I take

care of the executives around me, usually the assistants take care of the work themselves." He turns away which signals the end of the conversation.

"Okay." My lips quiver in a shaky smile as I try my best to hold it together. All the while, my insides feel like they are being pulled outside my body—a centrifuge of anger.

The only way I know how to deal with difficult situations is directly, so I call

Bree back.

"Look, we have to figure this out." Is the most I can muster. "I need to be in the loop. Now, I've experienced some times when you've deliberately kept me out of the flow of information."

"Sarah. I'm just doing my job." Bree sounds frighteningly calm.

If Bree has talked to Grace and Karsen, I'm almost certain they've gossiped about me. I feel like the entire world is looking right into my soul. Sending the calls to voice mail, I walk straight to the restroom, enter the stall, sit on the toilet seat and stare up at the cracked, peeling paint on the ceiling. Look at this. Look where I am. I'm hiding in a bathroom stall again. *Do not cry. Do not cry.* Is this what things have come to? Am I so in need of social validation that I have to hide? I get up, open the door, walk to the sink and stare at myself in the mirror.

Grace and Karsen have started ignoring me. So, as I walk past their offices, it's as if I don't even exist. Returning to my desk, I do my best to fix the errata in the contacts for the eighth time. IT assures me that it is not an "issue."

The rest of the day is a blur. If only I had some clever comebacks or even a hilarious way to trip Bree up, but it just isn't in me. I have always hated situations where I have to "mess" with someone else. Why not be honest? I'm pretty good at that.

I take a deep breath and dial Bree's line. "Listen Bree, I called because I want you

to know that I'm incredibly unhappy at this job, I've tried to work out our compatibility issues to no avail and if it doesn't improve, I'll have to contact HR."

"Okay."

No hedging, no nervousness. Just Okay.

"I'm not joking," I calmly say. "If we can't work it out, I'm contacting HR."

"Go right ahead." Bree's tone is even, clear, confident.

It chills me to the bone knowing that people like Bree exist. Those who continue to feed off of other people's kindness and continue to plunge ahead with no regard for humanity. Maybe that's my lesson in life. Here I thought I was the Executive Assistant expert, when really, all I've become is a doormat in a high traffic area on a Studio lot.

For the next few weeks, I interact very little Bree. When we do speak with each other we are cordial.

[AAAAH!]

One morning, as I sip my French Press French Roast, I gaze out my kitchen window. It's not a particularly special view, just a few palm trees and a post-war apartment building, and it occurs to me that I am in the same spot I was when I left Kansas City—unhappy and stuck. The solution could be the same. I grab my keys and go for a walk. If I am going to be unhappy, why not be unhappy in a place I enjoy.
Outside.

As I round the corner, I see Harper, the girl whose dog,

Gus, tried to make a snack out of my behind.

She waves from across the street.

Since its Sunday, there aren't many cars on the road, just people walking. It's a gorgeous, sunny November day and everyone is outside. On days like this, I enjoy calling a friend or two in Kansas City and talking about the weather. When I last checked, it was bitter cold with freezing rain in Kansas City and sunny and warm in California.

Double checking that Gus is safely locked inside the yard, I cross the street.

Harper meets me at her fence. Her house is small and quaint. It looks like she's done a nice job with the inside, but the outside could use a coat of paint and there is no landscaping.

"Hi…Harper, is it?" I say.

"Yes. And…Sarah," she leans awkwardly against her fence. "How's the, uh, injury?" She smiles at this joke and I smile, too.

"Fine, I thought it was worse than it was. It ended up being a mean bruise, but I survived."

"I can see that. Listen, what are you doing tonight? I was wondering if you'd like to go to dinner."

"Sure, I mean, I'm not doing anything. Okay. What time?"

"Seven thirty? I'll come to your door and we can walk somewhere close."

"Sounds good. See you then."

I wave goodbye and continue to stroll down the sunny street. Harper seems harmless and friendly. I sounded so awkward. 'Sure, I mean, I'm not doing anything. Ugh.' What an imbecile. I could use a nice friend in the neighborhood.

Harper knocks on the door at 7:32pm. She is dressed in

shorts and a golf shirt. I decided to wear jeans and a flowered top. Good, we're both casual. Nothing embarrasses me more than being over or under dressed for a date. I lock the door behind me and we head out toward an area where a few restaurants are located.

"How do you feel about Sal's?" she asks.

"I love Sal's," I say. "I'm really hungry." I'm looking forward to some nice conversation.

Sal's is a casual restaurant in a pleasant shopping area. We are seated in a booth in the corner and, as I slide in, I'm amazed at how comfortable I feel around her. I order red wine and she orders a beer. We sit silently looking at our menus. A chatty blonde waitress comes by and takes our orders and menus leaving me to face a vast chasm of potential conversation. I am glad I picked something easy to eat, salmon. It's not necessarily my favorite thing to order, but I know it poses the least risk of spillage. Next to being over or underdressed, spilling on my clothing is the worst thing that can happen on a date.

"So..." Harper breaks the silence. I like that she ordered a steak, medium rare with fries and a salad with blue cheese. This comforts me for some reason. Steak is a dependable meal, a no nonsense decision. "I see you run quite a bit, have you even done any races?"

"No, but I'd like to." I've never thought about doing a race before, but it sounds

like the best answer. The conversation meanders around simple subjects and eventually comes to exes.

She is an architect, 35 and once lived with a woman who was a painter.

I can feel my armpits sweating under my blouse. Damn my deodorant! I make a mental note to change brands. Then, I quickly pull both arms close and touch my chin in a thoughtful gesture. Hopefully she didn't notice.

Harper continues to talk about her previous girlfriend.

Her name is Carol. That lasted three years and they broke it off about two years ago. Now she's just dating. We talk about what it is like to live with someone and I talk about Jill. I do my best to paint her in a fair light. It's hard, but I manage. Our dinner comes and we eat and chat. We've fallen into a conversational groove. It's all very civilized and calm. My salmon is surprisingly good. It has a very light cream sauce and the vegetables are sautéed with a bit of garlic but are still crunchy.

Every once in a while during the dinner, I catch myself looking at her eyes and the sparkle of her smile, then quickly brush it off. I really don't want anything serious right now. A friend would be perfect. This girl is way too bland for me. I need someone I can talk to about my problems and work successes, and most importantly, someone who can give me a different perspective. Yes, Harper will be my friend, my cute, sparkly-eyed and warm-spirited friend.

After dinner, Harper asks if I would like to walk around and window shop. I agree and we take a few steps. Suddenly, I feel her fingertips brush mine as we walk; and then I feel her fingers intertwine with mine. A rush of adrenaline goes through my arm and body and I smile inside. It almost feels more intimate than a kiss for some reason. It's been a long time since I have held hands with someone and it feels good. We walk along the sidewalk looking in at the merchandise and making little comments. We will never be just friends.

CHAPTER ELEVEN – LIVE YOUR DREAM

Months have gone by with no change in the tension level between Bree and me. I've found it best to just do my job and deal directly with Mr. Barlow whenever possible. This week, he's in New York. The phone rings as I settle into my desk one Monday morning in February.

"Mr. Barlow's office," I try to be as friendly and efficient sounding as possible. "Hi Sarah, I tried Bree but she wasn't there." It's Grace.

I've given up trying to explain that I am steps away from her and why wouldn't she call me or even walk by my office and speak with me, but I'm exhausted "What do you need?" I ask.

"My boss is organizing a surprise party for Brink's 55th birthday on Tuesday in

New York and we need Senator Eden's contact info."

The party is nowhere on the calendar, obviously, but I am stunned. An event, is being held which includes my boss and no one told me?

"I'll email it to you."

"Thanks." She hangs up quickly.

People have all but stopped dealing with me and the hardest part is that includes the people who are in closest proximity to me. There have been a couple of times over the last nine months when Bree is sick and I get a sudden flood of information. It's at those times, when my blood boils and I try to contact people and explain that I should be included on the distribution list or contacted with information or just included in the flow of information.

It's almost as if every few months, Bree undoes all the work I have tried so hard to build. Forwarding the phones to voicemail, I leave for lunch. The commissary is surprisingly slow and I end up chatting with the deli worker, Serge, I find out he has been battling cancer. Despite his health issues, he looks well but, I can tell he is worried, though. It pains me to think that he is going through this. There isn't enough time for me to continue talking with him because a line is forming.

I've ordered my favorite sandwich, avocado and cheese on rye with mayo, and leave. Yum. This is my favorite sandwich from the studio commissary and I savor it on the picnic tables underneath a beautiful arbor. I think of Serge. I hope he's going to be okay.

On the drive home, I think about my mother. Where is she and what could she be doing right now? Pushing away fearful thoughts that something horrible has happened to her, I imagine her walking through the Country Club Plaza. Shopping is one her favorite pastimes. As she browses the stores, she snuggles into her wool pea coat and scarf, kicking at stones in her path and nodding at the shopkeepers whom she knows. When I get home, there is a note taped to my door and a rose on the welcome mat.

> Sarah,
>
> You are invited to a birthday party for Gus. He is five years old and ready to party. No gifts necessary, but belly scratches encouraged. Come after 7 pm. (Gus has to have time to get ready.)
> Harper Dorsey

I unlock my door with a smile and throw my bags down. Then, I plop down on the sofa and sigh. This sigh is a good one.

Not like those other grief laden ones. I get up and go over to my desk, find the legal pad and write:

Bring it on. I'm ready.

I get up and change into some comfortable clothes. The last time I was at the store, I bought some dog biscuits for Gus. So I grab a few and put them into a gift bag to take over. I grab a bottle of wine from the kitchen and check my makeup. All I need is lipstick, a little powder and I'm good to go!

I walk over to Harper's place and knock. She probably doesn't hear me, so I open up the door and let myself in. Harper has reggae music playing and is cooking fried chicken, mashed potatoes and collard greens in the kitchen. This happens to be my favorite meal and I am impressed that she would attempt a dinner like this, since I told her my Grandmother used to make the best fried chicken I ever had. I give her a hug and open the dog biscuit bag for Gus who has come over to greet me and eagerly awaits his
treat.

Harper is stirring and humming. She opens the refrigerator door, pulls out a beer, opens it and hands it to me. I haven't felt this good in a long time. It's nice to have someone else plan something for a change. Harper looks great, too. Did she lose weight or change her hair? I can't figure out why she looks so attractive right now.

I ease into the kitchen chair and we talk about the day's events. Harper talks about some plans she is working on now for a home not far from our neighborhood. The landowner comes from a wealthy family and has a few homes in the US, but he plans on making this one his permanent summer residence. Putting my vow to not gossip on the back burner, I tell her about my strange encounter with Helga, the two-faced assistant, Grace, the back-stabbing friend and Bree, the bitch. Harper goes back into the kitchen and brings out my uncorked bottle of wine with two glasses. As she pours the wine, she tells me that she's dealt with people like that before and they usually aren't worth the time.

I agree with her. It's hard, though, for me to imagine that I lived in a world, where I really didn't see people for who they truly were. I have a theory about people like Grace. They have a repertoire of stories they draw from, and whenever a new incident arises they pounce on it, devour it then regurgitate it, over and over again, as entertainment for themselves and other people. They sit at dinner and try to work the person's name into the conversation so they can dramatically pause and say, "Oh, yes. I know all about HER." And then tell an unseemly, almost always embarrassing and tragic story about the person. All this preparation is for a few minutes of amusement and entertainment. In that same few minutes a single person is diminished and sadly replaced by a caricature.
No longer a human being, but one of those ridiculous drawings you buy for a dollar at the

local carnival.

Back in Kansas I learned about cows. They have sensitive stomachs and must regurgitate what they've eaten (called "cud") and re-chew it, over and over again, until it is easily digestible. I decide to call these gossipmongers "Cud Spewers" or maybe "Crud Spewers." I share this theory with Harper and she knowingly nods. As I continue on about Grace, something happens. I hear myself saying the words "bitchy assistant."

"Oh my God," I say, "That's me." My stomach drops. "I was a bitchy assistant. I just described myself–how I used to act. I used to gossip with them. No wonder I was so specific."

"Oh, I can't imagine that," Harper says warmly.

The more I relax, the more I talk about my work. I tell her how terrible my job has been. Harper doesn't seem to mind me prattling on and on. She doesn't offer any opinions either. When the dinner is ready, she makes a bowl of something for Gus and we all sit down to eat. Gus is on the floor next to the kitchen table. Harper and I look at each other and take in the warmth. I take a bite as she watches. The chicken is crispy outside and tender and juicy on the inside. I close my eyes and inhale. It is truly good. The potatoes are way too salty, but the collard greens are even better than my grandmother's. They are tender but still firm. My grandmother would cook them to death. What a great meal. I am more than impressed since I haven't even tried this recipe.

After dinner, we both do the dishes. Harper takes her turn at talking this time. She tells me how she bought this house a year ago, explaining the intricacies of her home loan. She was able to afford it only because she had a great loan person who worked the numbers for her. We sit on the couch and settle in. In the three times we've been out over the last month we have never kissed. The conversation lulls for a moment and there is a slight tension as we look at each other. I hate this moment. The first kiss is always incredible, but the moment before is excruciating.

I try to fill the tension with more chatter and just as I open my mouth to speak, Harper leans over to plant a kiss on me. She loses her balance and her lips bear the weight of the fall. It ends up being a much more forceful kiss than was intended. I'm so surprised I don't know what to say. She interprets the silence as positive and tackles me with a lip pressing, bone-crushing kiss. This time, I leap up and scream, "NO! This is not going to happen with you. No. You…are a friend…a good friend."

I rush to get my purse. And at the door, I turn back to a stunned Harper, who is still on the couch; shake my head and say, "NO!" for emphasis.

I walk as fast as I can across the street almost getting hit by a few cars. Before I can think, I'm inside my apartment with the door bolted. What in the world did I just do? I laugh to myself about my ridiculous reaction. I do like Harper but…she's just not my type. Not that I know what my type is, but she's just a nice girl. She's a friend, not a girlfriend. My mind races with a million questions. Will Harper call me or knock on my door to see if I'm all right or to talk? Did I scare her off with my sudden outburst? I've never had such a violent reaction to a simple kiss before. Every time I think of this, I chuckle. What a ridiculous response. I watch some television to relax and then go to bed. Harper doesn't knock or call that night.

The next day, at lunch, I shove a $50 bill under the ones in Serge's tip basket while he isn't looking. Not that this will make a difference, but it's the only way I can think to help, right now.

My voice mail light is on and a warmth overtakes me as I listen to the message. It is Harper and she doesn't mention my outburst but instead, asks me to dinner for tonight. My day flies by as I ride the warmth of that message.

That evening, Harper and I go back to Sal's. She is warm and welcoming and I

apologize profusely for my actions the night before. She shrugs off my explanation and we have a pleasant dinner together. The conversation veers to Harper's ex-girlfriend, Carol. Her parents are from Paris and she grew up traveling back and forth between Los Angeles and France. She talks about how Carol began and ended Harper's wine education in one single evening.

Early on in their relationship, Carol and Harper were out at a restaurant and the sommelier brought over a wine list and handed it to Harper. She looked at it for a long time and finally, Carol asked to see it. Looking it over, Carol said, "I see why you had trouble with choosing. They're all crap here." She called the sommelier over and asked if the restaurant had a private reserve list. When the list came, the sommelier handed it to Harper who immediately handed it to Carol. She chose an expensive bottle of which Harper had three sips. Harper said that she just can't understand wines and really doesn't like the taste.

"The wine she chose was disgustingly sweet and I really couldn't stomach it." On the way home Harper confessed that she hated wine and although Carol was appalled, she kept it to herself.

"It definitely was one of the things she brought up as we were breaking up, though," laughed Harper. "As she walked out the door, she said she couldn't live with anyone who had trailer park taste and a beer budget. I guess she expected me to go nowhere."

"Wait," I say, "what about the wine I brought last night? You drank that."

"It tasted fine to me. Or maybe it was the person who chose it," Harper smiles.

In the low light of the restaurant she looks much older. The lines in her face are accentuated. I try to imagine her thirty years from now. Would she still have this sense of humor? This spark? There is something about her...I can't put my finger on it. She just makes me feel so peaceful. I am more relaxed and peaceful than I have been in a long time.

The waiter brings the check and I grab it first. Harper starts to protest, but I say I would like to treat. She relents, but begrudgingly. After all, Harper says, she invited me to dinner. This is a thing I love to do. It puts me in the driver's seat on a date. I've even gotten into fights with women in the past that did not want me to pay for dinner or lunch. For me, the idea of treating someone to a meal is thrilling. It gives me a sense of purpose and worth.

On the walk back, we stop at a furniture store. It is closed, but there are several sofas on display. Harper points out her favorite. It's a big comfortable leather one, with big arms. She says she's also been looking at the end tables for a while. I smile to myself. This was the sofa I had chosen as I was mentally redecorating my apartment. Harper stops walking and turns to me, "Hey, you're tall!"

Shifting on my feet I explain, "It usually takes people about two or three meetings with me to get my height. I believe there are short tall people and tall short people. I fall into the second category."

We turn and walk in silence and Harper takes my hand. We hold hands all the way back to my apartment. I fish around in my purse, pull out my keys and look up to find Harper's lips inches from mine. I see my reflection in her eyes as she puts both arms around my waist and pulls me into a soft and lovely kiss. It's the kind of kiss I like to call "The Loop." Better sometimes than sex, this type of kiss remains in a loop continuing to replay in my mind throughout the following day. Harper silently leaves and I float inside then walk over to the Mary Shrine, kneel down and begin:

Dear Mary,

I haven't felt this good in such a long time. Please don't let this end. I can't take another heartbreak. All I want is a peaceful loving relationship. I'm so tired of being alone and making the same mistakes.

I get into bed, turn the light out and think of Harper and the kiss. What is she doing right now? Is she brushing her teeth? Cleaning her ears? Is she thinking of me? Ugh. I have got to stop this sappy thinking. This is what gets me into trouble all the time. The best thing to do is to focus on my career.

[SCRATCH, SCRATCH, SCRATCH, SCRATCH]

It's a Thursday and today, I notice that all activity and flow with regard to my job has stopped. The phone barely rings and, unless Mr. Barlow is in town, which he isn't, I rarely speak with anyone.

It is then that I decide to write. I use longhand with short quick strokes. After the first sentence I look at my handwriting. It looks just like my mother's. Strange how my mother always taught me to make my mark and yet here I sit and 1 am without a clue as to how to do it. Another thing my mother taught me is that relationships with men don't help anyone make her mark they only impede the process.

I write:

> I got my first taste of how things should be when my mother came home from work and showed me her paycheck one day. I was ten years old and I'll never forget how proud I felt of her. She told me that she earned the money and could spend it any way she wanted to. That night, my mother and I watched the Mary Tyler Moore Show. I watched with a new perspective because I now understood how important it was for Mary to take care of herself. It wasn't just a necessity; it was a privilege that offered rewards. Mary was able to go on vacations, even if she had to scrimp and save. She was able to buy beautiful clothes and date good- looking men. As I watched Mary talk with her boss and interact with her best friend, Rhoda, I knew I would be like that one day. No man was going to tell Mary what to do. That's what my mother told me my father did. Mary offered a safe place for me to dream about the future and protect myself from the present. If I focused on the future, the present wouldn't hurt as much. I think I was also worried about my father returning from a drinking binge at a bar. The last time he did that he screamed at my mother and me for an hour, went into the kitchen and smashed a vase my mother had sitting in the sink, ran to the bedroom and passed out on the bed. He woke up the next day without recognition of any wrongdoing.

> That happened a lot with my family. I woke up to a morning filled with cheery smiles and "pass the eggs, please" with no mention or apology for the

frightening display the night before. No wonder I live in a fantasy world.

[BLINK, BLINK]

The title hits me first as I peek into my workbag for something to read. "Me" is typed at the head of the well-worn pages, which are bent and broken from being roughly shoved into the "Purge File." My hands tremble and as I pull the stapled pages out, a corner tears off.

> My Mother is my best friend. If you saw her, you would think she was my sister. It's really funny to see men come on to her and then ask if we are roommates. I remember the first time she came out to LA to visit. A friend of mine, Matt, took us out to eat at a very nice restaurant on Melrose.
>
> We walked around a bit and went into Wacko, a little novelty store. She bought a little wind up toy and then we left. As we got onto the curb, I saw her pull something out of her bag. The next thing I know, she's squirting silly string all over us! I couldn't believe it. We had a great laugh about that. Then we returned to the valet stand to pick up Matt's car and decided to go to a club. While we were waiting, my Mother squirted the valet and the man next to her with the silly string. Squirming uncomfortably, I watched her giggle with glee as the silly string covered stranger leaned in close to her and whispered something I couldn't hear. The next thing I know, she hopped into his car and they left.
> Not many Mothers will do that.

We've always been close. When I was seven years old, we'd go on "dates"

> together. It would be just the two of us and we would go to the Leopard Room in the Ramada Inn and talk about "girl stuff." I used to tell her everything. Girls, school, everything. In fact, I'd feel guilty if I didn't tell

her something that happened to me.

One time she had to go to work early so she left me at home with instructions to go to her friend Sheila's house at half past eight.

Unfortunately, I was six and couldn't tell time. I waited what seemed an eternity and went to Sheila's house, but Sheila's told me she couldn't watch me and sent me to the bus stop. I went there, probably a half an hour early and waited, but the bus never came. I panicked and stuck my thumb out and a man stopped in a car. I knew it was wrong, but I had to go to school so I got in.

When I got home from school I sat in a chair, sucking my thumb with my favorite blue blanket wrapped around me. She walked in and said "What's wrong?"

She always knew what was wrong with me. It was almost like she could read my mind.

She shared some doozies with me too. I remember the first time she was dumped by a married man. I was seven years old and I came in from playing outside. It was a hot summer's day and all the windows were open.
Helen Reddy's "You and Me against the World" was playing on the record player and Mom was sitting on the hardwood floor crying. I just went over to her and she grabbed on to me and held me tight. Then she gave me the best piece of advice I've ever heard —"Never get involved with a married man." She said, "It's just you and me in this world."

SINGS LIGHTLY: "YOU AND ME AGAINST THE WORLD"

She was right about that. My father left when I was three. I had nightmares about his drunken rages for years after he left. He never paid a day of child support and my mother and I lived in poverty for the first six or seven years of my life. Oh, but you don't want to hear about that. My Mother is a much more pleasant subject.

She was always such a cool Mom too. She loved the same kind of music I liked and we used to sing along to Linda Ronstadt as we cruised around looking at cute men.

She used to tell me all about being abused by her parents as a child and how lucky I was to have a Mother who loved me. I feel quite fortunate to have such a contemporary Mother.

When I was young, I used to leaf through the pages her college yearbook until I found her picture. She was homecoming queen that year and had on a shiny tiara and a very happy smile.

And you'll be happy to know that I have carried on that tradition. (TAKES

OUT TIARA AND PUTS IT ON) I was elected Prom Queen! My mother has never aged, she's always been conscious of her appearance. Maybe that's why, now, when someone asks if she has a daughter she says "no." She also used to tell me she had no friends.

Of course she had friends. We used to go over to her friend Barbara's house and they would talk and talk. Barbara's husband, Joe, was an alcoholic who would periodically say to me, "When you grow up your ass will attract a lot of men." She would let me stay overnight at their house and play with her kids. It was kind of fun to pretend to be a part of a family. They all seemed to have their quirks, but they were an entire unit. My

Mom and I were only a fragment.

My secret wish became to have a family. Nothing too elaborate. Just a father and maybe a brother or sister (but I didn't want to press my luck). I had for a time wished for a chimpanzee, but then I met my teenage neighbor's spider monkey that screeched every time I moved). So, every birthday cake, every star, every penny I could throw into a fountain I wished I could have a father. He would be the super dad I'd never had before. Not like the last one who left without saying good-bye. Or who took me to bars when I was five. My Mom would go on dates and I would wonder, is this "the one?" Usually they weren't around very often, but occasionally one would stay for a while. But, none stayed long enough. The only problem was, well, I was a little messy. So. my Mom did the most wonderful thing—she sent me to an organizational therapist who asked me all kinds of questions but never really offered any solutions. I'm still messy, but I've accepted it.

College was the best thing that happened to me!

The day after graduation I was a sitting in the kitchen:

MOM: I found an apartment and I'm moving there next week.

SARAH: A week? My God, I don't know if I'll have time to pack.

MOM: I'm going alone.

SARAH: I can't come?

MOM: No.

SARAH: Oh. (MOM TURNS AWAY) Mom?

She left the next day.

I told you I'd never leave. I didn't cry. I was the strong one and look what it got me. I'm a basket case.
You were never there to say "it's you and me" it was JUST ME!! IT WAS

ME AGAINST THE WORLD.

The last time I saw mom was last year, but we talked on the phone about six months ago. She said that she'd lost her job and her apartment. When mom asked if she could come out here to LA and live with me, I said,
"No."

I was hoping when I moved away I could get on with my life. But instead I wake up every morning and wonder if I can make it. I wonder if today will be the day that I scream at my boss or ram into the fucking slowpoke in front of me on the 10.

Before I realize what I'm doing, I am tearing the pages I've just read, throwing them on the ground and stomping on them, screaming, "Fuck you, MOTHER! Mother fucker!"

My downstairs neighbor does not take kindly to this and begins to bang on the ceiling.

Crawling into bed, I imagine I am a cosmic dust pan, moving through time and space, sweeping up all the specks of dust I have become over the years.

It's been almost a year since I started working for Mr. Barlow and the troubles with Bree have only increased. I draft an email to Kathleen from HR. Surely, a department called Human Resources will be just the place to find a human to help with this seemingly insurmountable challenge.

Hi Kathleen,

I would like to file a formal complaint with regard to my work environment and coworker, Bree Gray.

Over our time together, she continues to:

-        Misrepresent our roles – telling people she is in charge of all major decisions in office

-        Undermine my work authority

-        Create a toxic and confusing work atmosphere – there are people who have been told I have a different role than I have.

Over the last year, I have attempted multiple times to clarify our roles with our boss Brink Barlow. When approached with the question of clarifying roles in our offices, Mr. Barlow said that I need to work it out with Bree. After seeing little to no change during my first exchange with Bree, I spoke with Mr. Barlow again and he reiterated that I should work it out with Bree. I've tried numerous times to work things out to no avail.

I also spoke with Bree on the phone regarding our roles and working as a team on five different dates.

I've checked in with Mr. Barlow regarding the quality of my work consistently over the last year and he is pleased with my performance.

This ongoing issue is affecting my health and personal well-being and I wish to rectify it immediately.

If you have any further questions, I can be contacted via email or numbers below.

Sincerely,

Sarah Marks

Carefully, proofreading and honing it down takes about an hour, but when I hit send, I know I've done the right thing.

I get ready for bed, lie in the dark, think of all the stupid, idiotic things I've done in the name of "finding the truth." I shift around in my bed and finally get up and walk to my full-length mirror. Sitting in front of it, I gaze at myself "Who the hell do you think you are?" The silence is deafening. I am cemented in this spot unable to let go of my now blurry image. Tears stream down my chin and drip onto my faded "Hang In There Baby" sweatshirt, complete with kitty swinging from a branch.

"I hate you," I say to my image in the mirror.

Then nothing. No silence, no heartbeat, only a slow building tension in my chest that, until now was buried deep, so deep I had mistaken the tension for nothing. I sit with this "nothing" as it builds a home in my chest. It lingers there like a squatter—no reason to leave and hanging on for dear life.

[BANG, BANG, BANG]

"Open up!" As I leap up, I catch my little toe on the edge of the bed.

"Ohhh," I scream-whisper "fffffffuuuuudge..." I hop to the door, fling it open and gape at my bloodied, non-friend neighbor.

"I've been mugged...need to use your bathroom." Non-friend neighbor pushes her way into my apartment.

At first startled, and then angry, then sad, I watch this first-time visitor rush into

my bathroom and slam the door. We've never seen each other's apartments in the six years I've lived here and, except for the shared wall, we have virtually nothing in common. Nothing until now. The front door rattles from not being closed properly. So, I hop over to shut it and flop down on my tiny living room couch. What the hell is her name? Debbie, Debra, Gladys…shoot. This embarrassing, unfamiliar familiarity grants me a feeling of achy discomfort and guilt. I should know this woman's name.

"I hate you," I cradle my throbbing toe and rock back and forth.

CHAPTER TWELVE -
THE NEW PATH

The sun rises over the Santa Monica Mountains on this New
Year's Eve morning.

I hike up the steep Paseo Miramar trail into the emerging
sunlight, then take a moment to catch my breath and look back
at the sweeping view of the Coast. A hazy mist is huddling in the
canyons and a hawk circles his prey somewhere below. I close my
eyes and breathe in the misty morning air, then turn to continue
the hike and kick at the dusty earth. I can feel the sun on my
face and the shady coolness on my back. The contrast gives me
chills. When I get to the vista, I have a three-sixty view of the
surrounding mountains and coast. The water down below is
sparkling in the, just risen, sun. I take a towel to sit on and some
water out of my backpack.

All along I have looked to other people for their advice. I
think back to the incident with Bree. Never before had I stood up
for myself. Maybe I do have what it takes to be successful. Maybe
I'm not stupid. I pull out the Tibetan bells, ring them and close
my eyes.

Getting up from my towel, I walk over to the edge of the
cliff. The water swirls around the rocks below and I follow the
glistening sea right out to the horizon. I'm all alone on the cliff
top as another hawk circles overhead.

I grab the paper sack containing the laminated picture of
Mary Tyler Moore along with the other shrine items and prepare
to throw. This shrine moved with me from city to city. As I fling

the bag as far as I can out into the ocean, I notice that it barely makes a splash. I take another deep breath and slowly let it out.

On the hike back down the mountain, something is missing and I can't quite put my finger on it. Then I realize I have not fantasized at all today. No trips down memory or rather, nightmare lane. No fabulous earth shattering discoveries. Nothing. I hike in silence. I hear the birds and the wind rustling in the trees. Were these things there all the time? How could I have missed them? My mind was so cluttered with stories and chatter that I couldn't hear anything. It's almost like someone turned the sound on after the mute button on a remote control was on.

I get home, shower and dress in a comfortable cotton blue shirt and some warm soft sweats. As I come out of my bedroom I am shocked by the absence of my Mary Shrine. I stop and take in the newly found space and shift my kitchen table over a bit. I am just about to start my coffee ritual when the doorbell rings. Looking through the peephole, I notice a woman dressed in a knit hat with a smart suit on. She looks to be about my age and seems non-threatening, so I open the door.

The woman thrusts an envelope out to me and says, "Sarah Marks?"

I nod, dumbfounded.

She continues. "You have been served by the attorneys of Regal and Ray." She stops for dramatic effect then continues, "Please be advised that your rights to counsel are up to you and are not obligatory under the California State Law."

I take the envelope and stand in the doorway well after the woman has gone. Then, I close the door. Sitting at my shrineless and now much roomier kitchen table, I open the envelope. Inside is a summons to appear at the Studio for a mediation meeting the following Monday.

As I read the thick, bound legal writ, I finally see the name "Lance Cheroux" at the top and "vs. Sarah Marks" and the words "Trebacon" buried in the text. Attached are three articles from trade magazines: Daily Variety, The Reporter, and Electronic Media. Each article mentions Lance Cheroux's questionable accounting methods and hints that he has been doing this for up to three years.

Spreading the papers out on my kitchen table, I read how the writ describes, in excruciating detail, my unstable upbringing. The studio has a pending lawsuit against Mr. Cheroux. I notice that the years the trades mention are the exact years that I worked for Mr. Cheroux. Lance Cheroux is in deep. So deep in fact, he dragged me into his mess by suing me for contributing to his demise by "creating an unstable and hostile work environment."

My father's drunken words reverberate through my head:

"You've already ruined Sarah for life. She'll end up just as crazy as you."

I'm, once again, haunted by the memory of my father grabbing my mother and shoving her into a glass plant shelf sending it crashing down—narrowly missing me. My heart pounds as I feel like I did back then, frightened for my life. I grabbed the closest heavy object—an iron trivet —and heaved it up. The metal disk clipped my father's left temple and sent him hurling toward us, face first.
Terrified, my mother and I scrambled out of the room.

So what if I reveal a deep dark part of myself? Would any of those people be as brave if they were confronted with this situation?

My eyes fall onto the envelope and scattered papers on my kitchen counter.

"I hope you are ready, Lance Cheroux," I say aloud. "Because I'm ready to face you." I gather the papers up, put them all neatly back into their designated order and place them into the envelope.

The following Monday, I am seated in the very conference room into which I used to bring coffee to executives, only now, I am three hours into a very intense mediation. I have been asked to take a seat next to my attorney, a friend of Harper's. There is a gum-chewing stenographer who makes little popping sounds as she records our words. The mediator looks like a well-guarded talk show host. He's good looking and before they start, he introduces himself as a retired lawyer and City Council member.

I look around and realize, except for the stenographer, I am surrounded by men.

Mr. Cheroux looks quite sleek in Armani, completely groomed down to his manicured nails. He sits with his hands crossed in front of him on the table and when I see that I am doing the same, I immediately switch positions. My hands go in my lap.

"Ms. Marks," Mr. Cheroux's attorney says, "you don't get along with many people at the studio. Do you?" He takes out a file folder clearly labeled "KRG Human Resources," and pulls out a call log. "Note for the record that on May 12th an employee in Ms. Marks' environs reported abusive yelling."

Is he talking about me telling the cubicle group to mind their own business?

"I…that was a reaction to an ongoing problem." Deciding to tone it down, I say, "My job has always given me a sense of pride."

The attorney holds up another folder. "Let the record show that this document is an email from Ms. Marks to Human

Resources dated April 7th of the following year. In it, there is a complaint logged regarding her dissatisfaction with her job. Do you recall sending this email, Ms. Marks?"

I can't believe this has come up and I glance over at my attorney for help. Isn't he supposed to say I don't have to answer the question?

Finally, I say, "Yes."

"We have six statements from others who say you were abusive to them and even tried to overtake their jobs. Were you ever institutionalized and is it true that you have a shrine to Mary Tyler Moore?"

I glare at my attorney who stares blankly out the door. "What does this have to do with the suit?"

"Your character is in question, right now, Ms. Marks. We have statements from many assistants that tell us that you were, let's say, not very courteous to them and you used your status to gain certain material items..." He glares at me over his reading glasses and adds, "like DVDs." The attorney pulls another folder out with two assistant's names: Grace Maletor and Karsen Baker. "Ms. Marks, both of these women tell us that you talked with them about your mental stability and the consequences it might have for
Mr. Cheroux."

For the first time in my life, I feel something I've never felt. It's almost like I have uncovered a part of me I never knew I had. And now, I have the opportunity to rewrite at least a portion of my life by speaking my truth.

"I understand I may have been unstable during that time. I also know that I am a different person now. I am aware of so much more about myself. What I have discovered is I'm not so bad. I may have done those things, but I did not intentionally mean to hurt Mr. Cheroux in any way. All I wanted to do was to make a decent living. I believe I got a little too caught up in the actual job, and I so regret anything I said or did to hurt other people."

"Being sorry is quite nice, Ms. Marks. But it doesn't begin to bring back the pain and suffering, not to mention the loss of Mr. Cheroux's reputation—and potentially his career—incurred during your lapse of judgment and unusual lifestyle choices. Your hostility to your co-workers directly affected Mr. Cheroux's outstanding social prominence."

My lawyer has been staring at Mr. Cheroux's lawyer and the Mediator intently.

He almost looks star struck. The Mediator speaks in a radio voice "Let's take a break.

We'll meet back here in fifteen minutes."

They all get up to stretch and I head to the women's restroom, my only sanctuary right now. When I am finished, I duck into an empty conference room and am surprised to see Brink Barlow in a moment of contemplation.

"Hi, Sarah," Mr. Barlow says. "Tough break about Mr. Cheroux."

"Hi, yes," I'm surprised that Mr. Barlow knows what's going on—

I had told him that I needed a personal day off from work but didn't explain why—there seem to be no secrets when it comes to my life and work. As I start to leave, I change my mind and decide to share more information with him, as he seems the only person interested in my side, right now. "We're doing the mediation in Conference Room One."

"What a coincidence," Mr. Barlow says "I have business in there, too."

He drops his paper cup of coffee in the trash, turns once more to look at something out on the horizon out of the window and walks out the door. Opening the door a crack, I watch Mr. Barlow approach the conference room. I stealthily follow a few steps behind; no one seems to notice as I slip into the conference waiting room. Then, I put my head down and listen as Mr. Barlow approaches Mr. Cheroux, whose attorney moves away to speak with the Mediator.

"Hi Lance. How's it going?" It's just Mr. Barlow and Mr. Cheroux now. "Looks like we're going to win this one, Brink." Lance cocks his head toward his attorney, "I only get the best in the business."

"Of course, you do, Lance. And I know you managed to get your numbers just right, as well. Well, I'm off to a meeting." He gives a nod to Lance and starts to leave, but turns back, "Oh, you may know the company. Trebacon. Seems they have been pirating movies through China and trying to launder them through studio executives. Of course, no one I know would be stupid enough to accept the offer. After all, Piracy is a Federal offense."

Mr. Cheroux shows only a brief jolt of recognition before quickly recovering. He even starts to speak but thinks twice about it. It appears that Mr. Barlow has spoken volumes. Lance gives a haughty upward nod to Mr. Barlow as he moves toward the exit and I suddenly see him in a completely new light. Forever trying to perfect his image, he has succeeded a little too well. Lance, I now see, will do anything to succeed—including throwing me under the bus. He is now at his lawyer's side and they are tittering back and forth.

Mr. Barlow nods gently toward me, as he quietly departs.

We all file back into the conference room and the Mediator speaks. "It looks like

Mr. Cheroux has had a change of heart. This case is over."

My lawyer looks relieved. Lance Cheroux looks crestfallen. I was his scapegoat.

Mr. Barlow is my savior.

I walk back to my car, all the time looking for Brink Barlow so I can thank him.

But he is nowhere to be found.

There is a note on my car, which reads:

Take the day off, Sarah. You deserve it. - Brink

The first person I want to share the news with is Harper. As I approach her door, I hear the enthusiastic barks of Gus. When Harper opens the door, I meet her gaze, a smile spreading across my face, and I embrace her, wrapping my arms around her sturdy shoulders. In that moment, I feel an overwhelming surge of affection, and I kiss her passionately. She playfully protests, saying, "No! No!" and we tumble onto the couch together.

This is unlike anything I've experienced before. As our desires intensify, I fumble with her shirt while she undoes my pants. I attempt to undo her pants, but my hand gets tangled in the armhole of my shirt, causing us to collide and bump heads. "Oof," we both exclaim as we tumble off the couch and hastily make our way to the bedroom.

With each piece of clothing discarded, forming a trail leading to the disheveled bed, we communicate without words, letting our bodies and desires guide us. The sunlight casts a shimmering glow on her hair, back, and legs, making her resemble the enchanting Betty Page, a stunning pin-up model. Unable to resist, I playfully nip at her nipple, eliciting a delightful "Ouch" from her as she grabs my backside.

We make love passionately and repeatedly, our connection growing stronger with each intimate encounter. I find myself counting aloud, whispering, "Fifth time," "Sixth time," as our desires intertwine. By the eighth time, exhaustion finally overtakes us, and we fall into a deep slumber. My dreams are a medley of galloping horses and people wearing mismatched shoes...

I wake up at six in the morning and gently kiss Harper, her hair disheveled on one side, and faint imprints of the sheets marking her left cheek.

"I'll make some coffee," Harper offers, as she reaches for a teakettle on her stove, removing the lid and filling it with filtered water. She places the kettle on the burner and retrieves a large French Press pot from the cabinet above the sink, a detail I hadn't noticed before. From another cabinet, she takes out coffee beans, expertly grinding them with a grinder. The comforting aroma of freshly ground coffee permeates the air as Harper carefully measures enough for eight cups. She grabs a well-seasoned frying pan, eggs, and cream cheese from the refrigerator, cracking the eggs into the skillet and skillfully scrambling the ingredients.

"Tell me something," Harper says, placing a couple of slices of yesterday's baguette into the toaster oven. "You obviously didn't kill your father since you discovered his obituary just a few months ago. I'm sure you've never been to a psychiatric institution either. So, what really happened?"

I gaze at Harper, captivated by the sunlight dancing in her hair, and respond, "My father suffered a severe injury but survived. However, we never heard from or saw him again. As for the 'loony bin,' well, maybe I did spend some time there. I was sent to live with my grandmother, but only for a few months."

Stirring the eggs with a spatula, I continue, "Now let me ask you something. Initially, I wanted us to be friends, no matter what. Yet, here we are, together. What changed?"

As the kettle whistles, Harper turns off the burner and

expertly pours the boiling water into the French Press. She stirs the mixture and places the plunger but refrains from pushing it down. She serves the scrambled eggs onto two plates, placing a piece of toasted baguette alongside each serving. With the plates in hand, Harper carries them to the table, and I grab the French Press, two mugs, and two forks. We settle down, taking our seats, ready to indulge in the breakfast she has prepared.

Harper takes a mouthful of eggs, savoring the flavors before looking at me with a gentle expression. After swallowing her first bite, she simply says, "You were never meant to be just a friend to me."

Her words hit me, carrying a depth of meaning that resonates within my core. I pause, letting her words sink in, and a warm smile spreads across my face. The connection between us, which began as friendship, has now blossomed into something far more profound.

As we continue to enjoy our breakfast together, basking in the quiet intimacy of the moment, I can't help but feel grateful for the path that has led us here. The aroma of coffee fills the air, intertwining with the warmth of our connection. With each sip, I savor the taste and the realization that this encounter, this unexpected journey, is a testament to our shared desire and the depth of our connection.

In that tranquil morning, surrounded by the gentle sunlight and the comfort of being with Harper, I feel a sense of liberation. The dreams that fill my nights have always held a glimmer of hope, a place where optimism thrives. Now, as I sit beside the person who has become so much more than just a friend, I am reminded that breaking free doesn't solely lie within dreams—it also resides in the choices we make and the connections we embrace.

With every sip of coffee and every exchange of glances, Harper and I continue to forge a bond, one that transcends the confines of mere friendship. We share our stories, our vulnerabilities, and our desires, creating a foundation built on trust, passion, and the freedom to be ourselves.

In this moment, as the morning unfolds and possibilities stretch out before us, I can't help but feel an overwhelming sense of excitement for the future—a future we will navigate together, hand in hand, as we continue to discover the depths of our connection and the boundless possibilities that lie ahead.

We make love one more time and I float home to get ready for work. Before walking upstairs to my apartment, I go to my mailbox. I forgot to get the mail last night and my mailbox is jammed full. As I walk up the stairs I sift through the bills and junk mail. I open the door to my apartment and kick it shut behind me. Thumbing through bills and a few fliers, I throw it all on the kitchen table and go in to my bedroom to dress and put on my makeup. I pick my favorite shirt, a pink knit with a black skirt and black shoes. This outfit makes me look like I feel–fabulous and free. I grab my purse and briefcase and head outside. As I step out the door, I notice an envelope, which was most likely left by my non-friend neighbor who received it in error. I step back inside and grab a sticky note and write:

Dear Debra,

Thank you. Hope you are okay. I will be home this evening and would love to talk if you have the time. Your friend, Sarah

I stick the note on Debra's door and look at the envelope, still sitting on my front door mat. It's from Lena Marks with the return address in Arizona. I pick it up, put it in my bag and head off to work. Looking up, I squint into the sunny cloudless sky and, in the white-hot light, I see clearer than ever before.

[THE END]

ABOUT THE AUTHOR

A creative spirit from a young age, 35 time award-winning author, Tricia Stewart Shiu experimented with acting and wrote one-woman shows and plays. She produced a short performance piece, DOING LUNCH, which eventually made its way into a short film trilogy that won "Best Dramatic Short" at the Houston Film Festival.

Shiu also directed a staged reading of a play she'd written called MARY, which was hosted by the Women's Artist Group of Los Angeles. That play eventually became the awardwinning novel, PLEASE HOLD.

Not only does PLEASE HOLD offer a rare glimpse into the world of top tier gatekeepers, it also serves as a reminder that spirituality comes in many forms and no one should judge another before knowing the full story. Everyone's journey to her own truth is layered and we all choose our path based on the highest form of guidance available. As we grow, so does our guidance.

In this quirky slice of life story, Shiu draws from her extensive experience as a veteran, high-level executive assistant at one of the top six entertainment studios in Los Angeles.

RAVE REVIEWS FOR
THE AUTHOR

★ ★ ★ ★ ★ "...yet another step up the literary ladder for Tricia. She is a delight to read and very quickly becomes addictive."
Grady Harp, Hall of Fame Amazon Top 100 Reviewer, Vine Voice

★ ★ ★ ★ ★ "In Please Hold, Tricia Stewart Shiu has created a female heroine whose journey is relatable to anybody who has ever struggled with the question of whom she is and whom she wants to become." **Jackie S.**

★ ★ ★ ★ ★ "Please Hold" is Tricia Stewart Shiu's most gratifying and relatable novel to date."
John Kelly, Cincinnati City Beat

★ ★ ★ ★ ★ "Tricia Stewart Shiu with each new book just gets better." **Denis Vukosav, Top 100 Amazon Reviewer**

★ ★ ★ ★ ★ A Must Read! "This is the very first book I have read from Author Tricia
Stewart Shiu and it won't be my
last!" **Monte F.**

★ ★ ★ ★ ★ "Tricia Stewart Shiu proved she was a good writer with her MOA book series.
"Please Hold" shows that she has strength writing in more than one genre." **Pam C.**
★ ★ ★ ★ ★ Another Great Book Written by Tricia Stewart Shiu." **Erica K.**

★ ★ ★ ★ ★ "Shiu culls much of the action in "Please Hold" from

her own life experience as a "veteran, high level executive assistant at one of the top six entertainment studios of Los Angeles." This first-hand experience allows her to write with razor sharp honesty and wit."
Emory D.

★ ★ ★ ★ ★ "Simply Enchanting!"
Ingrid L.

MORE BOOKS BY TRICIA STEWART SHIU

The Moa Series:
Moa (Moa Series, Book 1)
Statue of Ku (Moa Series, Book 2)
Iron Shinto (Moa Series, Book 3)

Gatekeeper's Guide Series:
Gatekeeper's Guide: To Ancient Essential Oils and Rituals
Gatekeeper's Guide: To Healing Stones, Elixirs and Rituals
Gatekeeper's Guide: To Planetary Alignments and Rituals

FOLLOW TRICIA AND LEARN MORE ABOUT PLEASE HOLD

Facebook: Please Hold
Twitter: Please Hold Novel
Website: TStewartShiu.com

"Having a dream is what keeps you alive.
Overcoming the challenges make life worth living."
- Mary Tyler Moore

ENDNOTES

[i]   Dialogue from "Love Is All Around," Mary Tyler Moore Show, Season 1, Episode 1. Air date September 19, 1970. Creators and Writers: James L. Brooks and Allan Burns.

[ii]   Dialogue from "Love Is All Around," Mary Tyler Moore Show, Season 1, Episode 1. Air date September 19, 1970. Creators and Writers: James L. Brooks and Allan Burns.

[iii]   Description from "Chuckles Bites the Dust," Mary Tyler Moore Show, Season 6, Episode 7. Air date October 25, 1975. Creators and Writers: James L. Brooks and Allan Burns. Writer: David Lloyd.

[iii]   "Love Is All Around." Theme song for the Mary Tyler Moore Show. Written and performed by Sonny Curtis.